All of a sudden Ephram felt like he couldn't take it anymore. He'd been tiptoeing around the truth about their relationship ever since he met Amy. He wanted it out in the open.

"Can I ask you something?" he blurted out.

"Sure."

"If Colin suddenly woke up tomorrow, you and I . . . would we become total strangers?"

"*Strangers?*" She drew back a little as if he'd offended her. "Ephram, I've shared more with you in these last few months than I've ever shared with anybody in my life."

"Yeah, I know," he said, feeling stupid for asking and trying to backpedal. "But—"

"You're the only person who's been here for me this whole time. You came with me to the hospital. You helped me convince your dad. And the way you stood up for me back there? You're the person who's gotten me through this."

Wow, Ephram thought. *That was pretty much the perfect answer.* It was hard to believe that he was sitting here with Amy, actually hearing her say how much he meant to her. He couldn't take his eyes off her.

"The way I see it," Amy went on, "if there's any miracle in my life right now, it's the fact that your dad looked at a map, and of all places, decided to move here." She turned toward him suddenly, and their faces were inches apart.

EVERWOOD

First Impressions

Adapted by Melinda Metz and Laura J. Burns
Based on the television series created by Greg Berlanti
and from the episodes "Pilot" and "The Great Doctor
Brown," written by Greg Berlanti; the episode "The
Kissing Bridge," written by Rina Mimoun; the episode
"Deer God," written by Michael Green; the episode
"The Doctor Is In," written by Vanessa Taylor; the
episode "We Hold These Truths," written by Joan
Binder Weiss; the episode "Till Death Do Us Part,"
written by Oliver Goldstick; the episode "Turf Wars,"
written by Rina Mimoun; and the episode
"Vegetative State," written by John E. Pogue

New York London Toronto Sydney

This book is a work of fiction. Any references to historical events, real people, or real locales are used fictitiously. Other names, characters, places, and incidents are the product of the author's imagination, and any resemblance to actual events or locales or persons, living or dead, is entirely coincidental.

SIMON SPOTLIGHT
An imprint of Simon & Schuster Children's Publishing Division
1230 Avenue of the Americas, New York, New York 10020
Copyright © 2004 Warner Bros. Entertainment Inc.
EVERWOOD and all related characters and elements are trademarks of and © Warner Bros. Entertainment Inc.
WB SHIELD: ™ & © Warner Bros. Entertainment Inc.
(s04)
All rights reserved, including the right of reproduction in whole or in part in any form.
SIMON SPOTLIGHT is a registered trademark of Simon & Schuster.
The colophon is a trademark of Simon & Schuster.
Manufactured in the United States of America
First Edition 10 9 8 7 6 5 4 3 2 1
Library of Congress Control Number 2003114489
ISBN 0-689-87082-5

EVERWOOD

First Impressions

PROLOGUE

"Ephram, you're gonna be late again."

His mother's voice brought him out of that place he went when we was truly in the zone. No, not a place as much as a state of being—perfect blankness.

Now he was aware of his fingers on the keys, the hard piano bench beneath him, the way the muscles in his arms and back moved as he played. Before, everything was blended, dissolved; there was no Ephram—just the music.

Abruptly he stopped playing and stood up. *That's probably the kind of crap Yanni sits around thinking,* he told himself, disgusted. He hurried into the kitchen and was surprised to see his father. At this time of morning, the world-famous surgeon Dr. Andy Brown was usually saving someone's life by doing some operation only he or God could do—

or at least giving an interview to *Time* magazine about it.

But today his father was sitting at the kitchen table. Ephram's little sister, Delia, sat across from him, Giants baseball hat on her head, her big brown eyes clearly filled with Daddy adoration. What was with her? The less their dad was around, the more she hung all over him.

"Good morning," his father said pointedly to Ephram.

Ephram avoided the table—and his father—and went straight to the counter. Out of the corner of his eye, Ephram saw his dad's shoulders stiffen when he didn't get a good-morning back.

"This mine?" Ephram asked, reaching for a brown paper lunch bag.

"It is," his mother answered as she handed him a glass of OJ.

"Someone's unusually quiet this morning," his dad commented. He really just wouldn't let go of the unreceived good-morning. Control freak. Anyway, Ephram was always quiet in the morning. There was nothing unusual about it. You couldn't know what was unusual if you had no idea what usual was. And you couldn't know what usual was if you were never around.

"Someone's unusually interested," Ephram shot back.

"Don't be nervous about tonight," his mother

said, tucking a loose strand of her brown hair back into its ponytail. "Your dad and I will be there to cheer you on."

"I'm sure," Ephram said moodily. He felt a pang of guilt. His mom shouldn't have to constantly try to make peace between his dad and him. For the millionth time he wondered why she bothered to lie for his father. It wasn't as if she were a trophy wife like a lot of the other doctors had. She wasn't Mrs. Dr. Andy Brown, who only came to life at social functions when she needed to help her hubby's career. People actually knew her first name—Julia—and she did a lot of things, like paint, just because she wanted to. So Ephram didn't get why she bothered pretending that his dad was going to show for the recital when he'd never come to one before. He'd had at least fifty opportunities and hadn't made it to a single one. Nor had he come to one out of fifteen birthday parties. Ephram could list at least a hundred "important" days his father had missed: the first lost tooth, the first T-ball game, the days other dads dragged out the video cameras for. Not that Ephram cared.

Ephram downed his orange juice in two gulps, put his glass in the sink, and gave his mother a fast kiss on the cheek, breathing in turpentine and oil paint and a little bit of the French perfume she always wore. "See ya," he told her. She smiled at him with one of her *we've got a secret* smiles.

He looped his backpack over his shoulder, gave Delia a wave, and headed for the front door of the apartment. He swung it open and stepped out, but he hadn't even closed the door before he heard his dad say, "His recital's tonight?" as though it was news to him.

"I've only told you ten times," his mother answered.

Ephram shut the door silently behind him. His mom didn't need to know he'd heard that little exchange.

"Piano man, I did a mix of 'Tears of Swine' that's guaranteed to get the band on the charts." Zack Cooper sat down backward on the piano bench, interrupting Ephram's preconcert warmup.

Ephram tried not to smile. Encouraging Zack was never a good idea. His friend was a big enough idiot as it was.

"You could be part of it, Ephram, my friend," Zack went on, as if his band wasn't really just a bunch of music geeks like himself. "You've already got the look goin' with that purple streak in your hair. Now, if you would give up on this classical crap and—"

"Mr. Cooper, my friend, unless you want to be forced to give up on this classical crap because you suck at it, I suggest you go get your cello and tune up," Mr. Gallager, Zack's private instructor, told him.

4

"How do you always manage to turn up at exactly the perfect moment? Did you have a chip implanted in my head?" Zack complained as he headed off after Mr. Gallager, giving Ephram a half salute.

Ephram returned his hands to the keys, but a thought slid into his head before he could start to play again: Is she here? *It's not like you invited her,* he told himself. *You big weenie.*

No. What Ephram had done was jam a flier about the recital into Catherine's locker. Then when she asked him about it, he'd muttered something about how the school orchestra teacher had said he'd give extra credit to anyone who went to the recital, which was true. But Ephram had actually wanted to invite Catherine. *Invite*—as in act as if he *wanted* her to go. Instead he'd acted as if he were just doing a chore for the orchestra teacher.

Ephram got up and meandered over to the curtain. *If she's here, it doesn't mean anything,* he thought. *Or actually, it means she wants to score some extra credit. Don't go thinking it has anything to do with you, not after the way you didn't even get close to asking her to come.*

He pulled the curtain aside a quarter inch and peered out, his eyes moving rapidly back and forth as he tried to see the whole auditorium at once. No Catherine. No Catherine. No Catherine. But in the spot where his mom usually sat, there were two empty seats. One for his dad—totally normal—but his mom's was empty too.

"Ephram," he heard his piano teacher say softly.

Ephram threw his hands up. "I know," he began as he turned around. "No looking at the audi—" The words died in his throat. He'd seen many expressions on his teacher's face: irritation, frustration, patience, affection, pride. But now Ms. Tollefson's face was blank, eyes flat, like melted marbles, melted blue marbles, and Ephram knew what she was about to say.

"What happened to my mother?" Ephram demanded. "Is she okay? Where is she?"

Even as he was asking the questions, he knew the answer. The big answer. It was on Tollefson's face. It was in Ephram's body. His guts had been replaced by snakes. Cold snakes that knew, as he knew.

His mother was dead.

He heard Ms. Tollefson talking, but it just sounded like a stream of unconnected words: "storm" and "accident" and "head trauma." The words meant nothing. Ephram's body knew the truth.

The snakes in his gut had disappeared by the next day, the day of the funeral. But the coldness in his belly remained, slowly numbing him.

His mother died yesterday. Yesterday, and he was

already at her funeral. His grandparents arranged it, he guessed. They were here, Grandpa Jacob and Nonny, crying. Ephram was wearing a yarmulke. So was his father. Ephram didn't remember putting his on. A rabbi said a prayer. Delia was crying.

The rabbi finished. Ephram hadn't understood a word he had said. He watched the coffin being lowered into the ground. His mother's coffin. Delia kept crying. The yarmulke itched. Ephram was crying too, though he hadn't realized it before. His shoulders were shaking and his face was wet with tears and snot. He must have been crying for a long time.

Should he have asked to see the body? Would that make it more real? He saw her yesterday. Yesterday. How did he get here? How did a hole form in the ground with his mother in it? A harsh, coughing sound escaped his father's lips—a single sob, like a bone breaking.

And then Ephram was pressed against his father's chest, Delia tight by his side. Warm. But it seemed nothing could warm the steady cold in his belly.

Ephram was sitting on the floor of his grandparents' apartment. The mirrors were covered. People were everywhere. Food was everywhere. He'd stuffed himself silly, but his belly was still producing that numbing cold. Maybe he should be glad to feel numb. But he wasn't; he loved his mother. He just sat there, watching his dad move from person to person, noticing the feel of smooth paint behind his head as he leaned against the wall.

Lying in bed, he wondered how many days had passed. He wasn't sure. He got up, he went to school, he talked to Delia whenever it occurred to him that she needed him. He didn't have to talk to the Great Dr. Brown much—he was back to the usual schedule of surgeries only he and God could perform.

The one thing Ephram didn't do was play the piano. He thought if he played, he'd be able to enter that blank place—the zone where he just blended with the music. But that would mean actively trying to forget. Maybe he couldn't feel, but he wasn't going to forget.

Ephram stared up at the ceiling. *What if my recital hadn't been that night?* he thought, over and over. *What if I had told her not to bother coming? What if Dad had been with her, just that one time? They would have been late, that's for sure. They would have—*

"Ephram! Delia!" his father called. "I need to see you both in the living room, please!"

What's he doing home? Ephram thought. *He's never home in the middle of the day.* Reluctantly he shoved himself off the bed and headed to the living room, taking his time. "What?" he asked after he took a seat next to Delia on the couch.

His father paced back and forth in front of them. "I have some exciting news. We're about to make a life change. Start an adventure."

Delia shot Ephram a worried look. He was right there with her—clearly their dad had experienced a psychotic break. What in the world was he babbling about? "An adventure," Ephram repeated slowly.

"A way-out-west kind of adventure. A clean-slate kind of adventure," his dad continued, picking up the speed of his pacing. "We're moving!"

"*Moving?* Where?" Ephram demanded, trying to get a look at his father's green eyes, almost expecting to see them twirling in his head.

"Everwood, Colorado," his dad answered, as if that made any sense.

"Where's that?" Delia asked.

"In Colorado, moron!" Ephram snapped. "Why are we moving there?" he yelled at his dad. The coldness in his belly had heated up. He wasn't numb anymore. He was mad.

"Someone told me about it once. They said it was the most beautiful little town they'd ever seen. It's on this hill . . . or is it a mountain?" his father continued.

Ephram rubbed his forehead with both hands. He felt like his brains were bubbling.

"Maybe it's on a hill by a mountain," his dad

9

went on. "Anyway, I was thinking last night that we should move there. What do you say?"

"I say that's not even a reason!" Ephram sputtered, words not nearly enough to express his outrage.

His dad threw out his arms, tilted back his head, and laughed. "I know," he exclaimed. "How great is that? We'd be moving someplace for no reason at all!"

"That's not great! That's crazy! That's Harrison Ford in *Mosquito Coast* crazy!" Ephram turned toward Delia. She needed to understand. "Harrison Ford took his family to the jungle and very bad things happened to them. Worse than anything in *Willy Wonka*. I'm talking nightmares for weeks."

Delia's brown eyes widened. "Dad?"

"He says crazy. I say it might be the sanest thing I've ever done," their father replied. "Now, of course I want this to be a democratic decision, so we'll take a vote."

Thank God, Ephram thought.

A calculating look crossed Andy's face. "Everyone who wants to move," he said, eyes flicking in Delia's direction, "*and* get their own horse, raise your hand."

Delia's hand shot up along with her father's, of course. "Well, that decides it," Andy announced with a grin.

"Democratic?" Frustration made Ephram's voice

come out in a squeak. "You just bought her vote."

Ephram's dad shrugged. "It's the American version." He started out of the room as Ephram leaped to his feet.

"And there's no conversation about the fact that I have friends here, and school, and one of the best music teachers in the country?" he demanded.

"I wouldn't be doing this if I didn't think it was the best thing for all of us," his dad answered. He left Ephram and Delia alone, the decision final.

Ephram flopped back down on the couch. "I want you to remember this moment," he told his sister. "This is the moment you conspired with a psycho to ruin what's left of our pathetic lives."

CHAPTER 1

Ephram stared at himself in the bathroom mirror. He'd fixed his hair so most of the purple streak didn't show, but it looked kind of lopsided. He wet his hands, shook off most of the water, and ran his fingers through his hair, spiking it up. Now it looked all greasy. He'd been messing with it for too long. He grabbed a towel off the top of the shower and scrubbed his head so hard he could feel his scalp burning. Then he threw the towel aside, tossed his head a few times, and did a light comb-through with his fingers. *Okay. Passable.*

He took a step toward the bathroom door and realized he'd forgotten to put on deodorant. *That* would really make a great impression on his first day at County High School. He could hear the girls now: "Yeah, I had a class with the new guy. Purple streak's cool. But the b.o., oh my *God*." Ephram slathered on the Right Guard, did another mirror check to make sure he hadn't done anything else stupid, like put his underwear on the outside, and then headed downstairs. He was just in time to hear Delia tell his father that she was pretty sure the school cafeteria wouldn't be able to change a fifty. Ephram snorted. How did his father manage to be brilliant and yet a total moron at the same time?

"Delia's off," his father said when Ephram hit the entryway. "C'mon, let's get you to school."

"I'm riding my bike." He'd never let his father— or even his mother—drive him to his first day at a new high school. *High school.* Even Delia wanted to walk to her school bus by herself, and she was eight.

"Why? I can drive you."

The moron part of his dad's brain was definitely in charge today. Apparently it had taken over completely ever since his father had decided to move them to this town.

"I appreciate the offer." Ephram spoke slowly for effect. "But you're about ten years too late." And he was out of there before his father had a chance to protest.

Ephram didn't bother to pedal fast. It wouldn't take long to get to the school. It didn't take long to get anywhere in Everwood. And he didn't mind a little time to look around. The mountains blew him away. And the sky. You never got to see sky like this

13

in Manhattan—not a big, wide stretch of it. Down in the Village, where the buildings were shorter, you could see a bigger chunk, but it was nothing like this. *Mom would love to paint—* He stopped mid-thought, his eyes filled with a sheen of tears again.

Should have seen that one coming, Ephram thought. His mother's absence hit him hardest when he wasn't expecting to miss her, like when he opened the package inside a new box of cereal. His mother could never open those; she always asked him to do it. The first time after she'd died and he'd started tugging on that hard-to-grip, not-quite-wax, not-quite-cellophane paper, hot tears had sprung to his eyes, and for a minute he hadn't been able to figure out why.

What if that happened to him at school? What if he smelled something or tasted something, or somebody said something, and wham! Tears. It's not like they came flooding down his face or even spurted out of his eyes. But they were there. You could see them swimming around if you looked close. *It doesn't happen every day or anything,* Ephram reminded himself. He'd just have to be on guard. If he could anticipate the response, he could usually stop it. It was just when he got hit unexpectedly . . .

Ephram suddenly realized the school had come into sight. The place looked like a ski lodge. Zack would die laughing if he could see it. Ephram turned toward the bike racks and pedaled over, taking in the groups of clones gathered in clusters here and there: all the guys with their short hair, all the girls with their perfect teeth and nails.

I'm definitely not in New York, Ephram thought as he parked his bike and locked it to the rack. In New York, people were always striving for individuality—whether through clothes, like Zack's vintage Hawaiian shirts, or hair, like Ephram's single purple streak, or rocking old school sneakers, piercings, tats, split tongues—whatever they could find to play with. Maybe they only *thought* they were screaming about their individuality, when they were really just screaming about how much they belonged to their own little group, like these Gap clones. But at least there was some diversity to keep things interesting.

"Freak, what happened to your hair?" one of the Gap boys said. "They were out of green at the store?" Ephram was already starting to learn to tell the clones apart. This one was a butthead.

Of course, a couple of the other Gap people turned around to see how Ephram was going to handle the situation. He didn't blame them. He especially didn't blame the incredibly pretty one with the long honey-colored hair, brown eyes, and an expression that seemed to say *I know he's a butthead and I'm sorry.*

Butthead moved closer, another butthead on his

15

heels. "My friend asked you a question. Where are your manners?" the backup butthead asked.

Ephram held up both hands, palms facing forward, in the universal symbol for "Hold on there." "Sorry. I didn't understand him. See, I don't speak Dumbass. But since you do, maybe you could translate for me?"

The clones watching started to laugh. And when they laughed, they started to seem less like clones. Ephram could pick out the laugh of the Pretty One. It was low, and kind of knowing. He liked it. He also liked the way both buttheads were having trouble with a comeback. Before they could come up with anything, Ephram slung his backpack over his shoulder and sauntered into the school. *Decent first impression,* he thought as he checked the slip of paper with his locker number on it, and then made a left, heading past a glass case filled with trophies and pictures of the football and basketball teams through the decades.

"Hey," a girl's voice called. The voice matched the laugh, and he turned around to see the Pretty One standing there, a smile tugging at one corner of her mouth. "You were pretty bold out there."

Bold. That sounded good. Not that he was going to brag about it or anything. He'd seen girls' eyes glaze over when guys got cocky. "It was just strategy, really," Ephram said.

She laughed, just as Ephram had hoped. He

didn't have a lot of experience with girls. But when he made a girl laugh, he felt like he'd done something right.

"Strategy?" she asked.

"I find it's best when dealing with any unfamiliar bully to strike early with the sarcasm." The words were just flowing out. He didn't know how it was happening, but he kept going. "It makes them wonder whether I have some secret butt-kicking prowess they're unable to detect."

"Wow." The girl raised her eyebrows. "You've really thought this out."

"Spend as much time in a gym locker as I have, you'll have a few theories of your own." Part exaggeration, part truth. All that time in front of the piano hadn't given him the best social skills.

"Were they really that horrible to you in New York?"

"How did you know I was from New York?" Ephram asked.

"That doctor who just moved here—he's your father, right?"

Not a topic he wanted to go into with this girl. "If you use the term 'father' loosely," he admitted.

"Ever since that article in *Time* about your dad giving up surgery to move here, it's all anyone can talk about," she told him.

"What do they say?" he couldn't stop himself from asking.

"A lot. Mostly they just wonder why he came," she said.

"If they figure it out, let me know." For the first part of their conversation, Ephram had felt like he and this amazing girl were in a privacy bubble or something. But now he was aware of people looking at them, at *him* mostly, but at the two of them together, too.

The Pretty One didn't seem to notice the attention. Or she didn't care. She was completely focused on him. "You really don't know why you're here?"

Ephram shook his head. "Whacked. I know."

"I think it's pretty wild," she said. "Sometimes I wonder if my dad's the most boring man in the world. He—" The bell rang, interrupting her. She took a step away. "Um, we should eat lunch sometime."

"Do you mean that as a philosophical idea, that people should eat lunch? Or do you mean that you and I should eat lunch together?" *Great, Ephram,* he thought. *It's clear you have inherited some of your dad's moronic qualities.*

The Pretty One smiled again, an all-out smile. "Together, of course." She started down the hall away from him.

This was so insanely cool. The Pretty One wanted to eat lunch with him. The Pretty One. He couldn't call her that. Yeah, that would be smooth. He'd lean against his locker. She'd walk by. He'd say, "Heeey, Pretty One. And she'd keep walking. "Wait," he called after her. "What's your name?"

"Amy Abbott," she answered. "And I like your hair."

"So, school, day one—I want to hear everything," Andy announced as he spooned sauce on top of Delia's spaghetti and moved around to Ephram.

"What brand is this?" Ephram asked, staring at the gunk now covering his pasta. "I think it might be past the expiration date. It's a little . . . moldy-looking."

"No brand. I made it," his father answered cheerfully.

Ephram looked at him, eyeing his newly grown beard suspiciously. *Perhaps it's the beard that's sucking all of the intelligence out of his head,* he thought. "Why?" Ephram asked, poking at a lump in the sauce with his fork.

"It's part of why I'm starting a family practice. I want to spend more time with my family. Cooking meals, eating together." Andy spooned a large helping of sauce onto his own plate.

"It does look kinda green, Dad," Delia said. She hadn't even bothered to pick up her fork.

"Vegetables. Green vegetables. Healthy stuff. Just give it a try," he urged her.

"Why don't you show her how it's done," Ephram suggested.

"Fine." Andy speared his fork into the spaghetti and twirled it around until he had a big wad of the stuff going. He shoved it in his mouth. Then without saying a word, he gathered all three plates and put them in the sink. "I think tonight we should order pizza," he mumbled through the unswallowed pasta.

"I have Mama Joy's on speed dial," Ephram told him, reaching for the phone. After he gave the order and hung up, he helped Delia with her homework while Andy did the dishes. In between subjects, his dad asked again about school.

Ephram gave him the stock reply: "Pretty good." Good in an Amy kind of way. That was pretty much his most successful exchange with a girl ever. And she just got cooler with every moment.

"Can you expand?" his dad asked.

"I'm a little ahead in everything but math, which is no biggie," Ephram answered. "Met a few people who might turn out to be of interest."

"Mr. Irv, the bus driver, said that we're going to get along good because Rosemary Clooney was playing on the bus when I got on, and he always knows how he's going to get along with people by what's playing on the radio when he meets them," Delia added.

"So you have a friend in Everwood already. That's great!" Andy said. Ephram hoped he didn't really think a bus driver counted as a friend for an eight-year-old. "Now I have some news of my own: I found an office today." He turned to Delia. "You're going to love this. It used to be a train station!"

"Really?" Delia asked in total Daddy's-girl mode, brown eyes sparkling.

"Uh-huh. Isn't that cool?"

The doorbell rang before Delia could answer. "Pizza. I'll get it." Ephram held out his hand, his dad slapped some money in it, and he hurried to the front door. Pizza could get cold fast in this town. He'd found that out the hard way. He swung open the door and saw a face he recognized from school. The expression on the guy's face made Ephram suspect the pizza boy fell into the butthead category. "What do I owe you?" he asked, hoping they could get through this with the fewest words possible.

"Heard your dad just bought an office in town," the pizza guy said.

"Yep. How much do I owe?" Ephram asked.

"Heard it was because the place smelled like his dead wife," the pizza guy added, smiling as he delivered the sucker punch. "Everybody in town's talking about it. Maybe you should tell your dad to act a little less whacked if he wants to get any patients."

What could he say to that? What the hell was he supposed to say to that? His first day wasn't even over and people had already moved on from

21

making fun of his hair to insulting his family.

"Well, she always did smell pretty good," Ephram said, just to say *something*. He squinted at the numbers scrawled on top of the box. "Here." He thrust a ten at the guy. "Keep the change." He grabbed the large pizza and slammed the door behind him. His neck felt hot and his whole face was burning. He couldn't tell if the sheen of tears had formed over his eyes or not; everything felt too hot. What was his father doing? Moving them to Crazytown and then proving to everyone that he was indeed certifiable? Is that what he and Delia were going to have to live with?

"Ephram? Pizza!" Delia called.

"Coming." Ephram stalked into the kitchen and dropped the pizza into the center of the table. "I'm going upstairs. I'm not hungry."

"I want us to eat together," his father protested.

"I'm not eating." Ephram continued upstairs to his room. He drew his first full breath only when the door was closed safely behind him. Was everyone going to know about this at school tomorrow? Was Amy going to treat him like some kind of freak by proxy?

Ephram closed his eyes, trying to push the thoughts out of his head. But he couldn't stop thinking about Amy. Would she have heard? What would she say?

• • •

Ephram came to a dead stop in the middle of the hallway when he saw Amy waiting by the cafeteria two days later, obviously looking for him.

"So how about that lunch, the nonphilosophical-with-me one," she said.

"Did you talk to my people?" Ephram asked. "My people handle me for lunch."

"Is that why I saw you eating by yourself yesterday?" Amy shot back with a grin.

"My people, my peeps I sometimes call them, they know I need my downtime," Ephram explained, already following Amy out the back door of the school. "So, no cafeteria?"

"*My* people made reservations elsewhere," Amy told him. "No looking down until we get to the top."

Why would he want to look down when she was walking in front of him? The sun turned streaks of her honey-colored hair to beach-girl blond. And the long strides she was taking as they climbed were somewhat hypnotic. He couldn't really look anywhere else.

"We're almost there," she said too soon. "You're gonna love this place."

"I'd love it more if it were indoors," Ephram answered. It was freezing out here. Not that he'd rather be anywhere else right now.

"Okay. You're ready. . . . Look."

He turned around. And he could see . . . everything. It was like flying. Standing still, flying.

"You can see the whole town from here," Amy continued. "There's Main Street. The grade school. The factories are all that way. Oh, and there's church row: Presbyterian, Episcopalian, Lutheran, Catholic, and Baptist."

"That's one holy street," Ephram answered, almost feeling as if he were swooping over it. "Where's the synagogue?"

"Are you Jewish?" Amy asked.

Ephram turned his gaze to her. "Half. My mom is . . . was."

Amy's eyes skittered away from his. "Sorry," she mumbled.

"About what?" he asked.

"I didn't mean for the topic to come up—"

"No big," he interrupted, wanting to get rid of her discomfort as quickly as possible. "Talking about her is unavoidable, what with her giving birth to me and all."

Amy nodded, and he could see she got it, that nobody's words brought on the pain. It was there. Always.

"I can't imagine what you've gone through, losing a parent." She reached out and touched him on the arm, so fast he hardly had time to let it register.

"Neither can I," Ephram admitted.

A tiny wrinkle appeared between Amy's eyebrows. "I don't get it."

"Maybe I'm still too close to it, but it never felt

like she died. Y'know, it still doesn't. It just feels like she's . . . not here. That's what you feel: them not being around anymore."

She nodded.

"So . . . lunch?" He reached into his backpack.

"What's that?" Amy asked.

Ephram looked down and saw a few books from his comic collection sticking out. "This? It's called manga. It's like anime. . . . You know, Japanese animation?"

"You mean like comics?" Amy asked.

Ephram felt a flush run up the back of his neck. Girls always thought manga was for losers. "Not really," he answered. "Manga is different from American comics in every way, shape, and form."

"Sounds geeky." Her nose wrinkled up and for a second she looked about Delia's age.

"Completely," Ephram agreed quickly. "It was a good-bye gift. I must've left it in here and forgotten about it."

"Did your dad really work on a king?" Amy asked.

How did we suddenly get on the topic of my dad? Ephram thought, the muscles in his neck and shoulders tightening. "He was just a prince at the time."

"What's it like having a dad who's famous?" She sounded genuinely curious, like one of his mother's friends asking about his father, all star-struck and excited.

"It's like this," he answered. "You're eight and he misses your birthday party. You want to cry about it, but he's on TV that night for separating the heads of Siamese twins. You're ten and he's not there to see you in the school play. He is, however, in the *New York Times* for helping restore the sight of a five-year-old kid. The prince you mentioned, I think of him as my dad's excuse for missing my elementary school graduation. You want to be mad at him. You want to hate him, but you can't. He was saving lives."

She was gazing at him with a sympathetic look in her brown eyes, and he knew it was time to ask the question. He didn't want to ruin the moment, but it would hurt less if he asked it today than it would if he waited until he was completely, pathetically in love with this girl. "Amy, why are you talking to me?"

"What do you mean?"

She sounded surprised. Sincere. That wasn't good enough. Ephram explained, "Where I come from, girls like you don't breathe near guys like me without a secret agenda."

"You got me," Amy said. Ephram braced himself. "Mine's world domination," she admitted.

They both laughed. "Should we sit down?" Amy asked.

They sat side by side, staring down at the town. Ephram's new home. "Seriously. You seem like you have enough friends. Why go out of your way to make me feel welcome?" Ephram asked, wishing he could drop it. He just couldn't forget that eager sound in her voice when she talked about his dad. Was she looking for a hit of secondhand fame?

"You have kind of a tragic-lonely thing going on. I dig it," Amy replied.

The tension slid out of Ephram's muscles. Now that was an answer that worked for him. Tragic-lonely he could deliver on his own. He took a bite of his sandwich.

Okay, she's kind of fixated on my dad, so she's not one-hundred-percent-absolute perfection, Ephram thought. *But she's here because she wants to hang with me.*

That *I can live with.*

CHAPTER 2

Ephram dried the dish in silence. He'd tried to convince his father that dish racks were a perfectly acceptable modern means of drying dishes, but his dad probably had it in his head that this father-son wash-and-dry session counted as "quality time." Not that they'd said a word to each other after the dish rack conversation.

Ephram would have liked to use this father-son time to tell his dad to keep his craziness contained to the house. Or at least make him aware of the fact that they'd only lived here a few weeks and more than a few people had heard at least one oddball Dr. Brown story; the latest was that his father had decided not to charge his patients any money for their visits. But he decided to stay out of it. If he went poking around in his dad's life, his father might think that gave him license to go poking around in Ephram's.

The sounds of tinkling on a piano pulled Ephram out of his thoughts. He shot a shocked glance at his dad, then followed the sound to the living room. Delia sat there, baseball hat low on her head, running her fingers up and down the keys. "Stop it," Ephram ordered.

Delia continued screwing around, her shoulders set, ready for a fight. "The piano just sits here," she complained. "No one touches it."

She was his sister. She was just a little girl. But the sight of her on that piano bench sent a wave of fury through Ephram. The piano was his thing with his mother. It wasn't just that he didn't want to play because he didn't think it was right to blank out and enjoy it. He didn't want to play because he wanted to save it as their thing, his and his mom's, and nobody else's. Ephram strode over to Delia and snatched her hands away from the keys.

"Dad!" she yelled, calling for backup. A second later their father was standing in the doorway.

"That's enough, both of you," he declared, scrubbing his fingers through his beard. "Delia, you go get washed up for bed. I'll be up in a little while to read to you."

"But I wanna—," Delia began, unwilling to give up.

"Go on," Andy told her. She gave him a look that said she wasn't happy, but she went.

When she'd reached the top of the stairs, Ephram's

father turned to him. "She has a point, you know. You're gonna have to play again sometime," said the man who had never made it to one of Ephram's concerts.

Ephram turned toward the piano and lightly ran his fingers over the curves of the music rack. "You're right," he said in a low voice.

His dad raised his eyebrows. "I am?" He sounded suspicious, with good reason. Ephram never said he was right about anything.

"Yes," Ephram continued in the same emotion-charged voice. "I must play again, Father. For it is only through the gift of music I can truly heal the pain that grows deeper within me." Ephram looked his dad straight in the eye. "Like you ever cared whether I played or not," he concluded in the disdainful tone he reserved for his father. Without giving Andy a chance to answer, he rushed up the stairs to his bedroom and shut the door behind him.

It felt good to be alone. As alone as you could get in a house with your family, anyway. He stretched out on his back and stared up at the ceiling, trying to imagine his room detaching and floating into space. His fingers twitched across his bedspread, but his hands clenched into fists as he realized he'd been silently playing his recital piece, the one his mother had never gotten to hear him perform.

If Ephram hadn't played in that one concert, his

mother would be alive. If she were alive, no Everwood. No Everwood. He'd still have friends. Music. A life.

He certainly didn't have a life now. The numbness that had hit him when Ms. Tollefson had told him about his mother's accident had never gone away. The only time it receded a little was when he talked to Amy. It wasn't even every day, but it was enough to keep him going.

Ephram made his way down the hallway, weaving through the between-class crowd. Just another hour to get through. Not that there was anything he was looking forward to doing after school. He opened his locker to do the book switch and a folded piece of notebook paper fell out and fluttered to the floor. It had "Ephram" written on it in flowery handwriting.

He picked it up, glanced around to see if anyone was watching him, and unfolded the note. It said: *Meet me after class. By the ski trail.* And it was signed *Amy*.

Ephram folded the note and shoved it into his pocket. Then he couldn't help himself—he shot his fist into the air like a pitcher making an out and started doing in a little dance. "I'm cool. Way cool. Meeting Amy. After school."

Bang! One of his books hit the ground. Had he just said "cool" out loud and done a jig? That was . . . so not cool. He took another look around. Amy was nowhere in sight. Thank God she hadn't seen that. The bell rang as Ephram grabbed the book he needed for his last class. He was meeting Amy in an hour.

An hour that felt like it lasted sixty hours, one hour for each minute. Finally the last bell rang. Ephram was the first one out the classroom door, first one out the back exit. He thought he knew where the ski trail was, but he wanted to make very sure he found it before Amy got there. Much as he wanted to sprint all the way, he had to slow to a trot. But that was okay. He wasn't a jock. He was the artistic brooding type, and with the altitude . . . Okay, he was panting. But he'd reached the path into the woods. Or at least *a* path. He'd been to the ski trail once, because there'd been nothing better to do. This was it, wasn't—

"Looking for Amy?" A blond guy Ephram had seen around school stepped out from between two trees, followed by the two buttheads who had greeted him on the first day. "'Cause she's not coming."

"Who are you?" Ephram asked. Usually he could come up with something better than that, but this surprise encounter threw him off.

"I'm her brother," the blond guy said. His cronies just stood there, slack-jawed. "I left you the note. I wanted to talk to you."

"You could have just *talked* to me," Ephram

said, getting a grip, although he couldn't stop himself wondering if "talk" was really a euphemism for kicking the crap out of him, what with the remote location and the goons. "You didn't have to go to the trouble of imitating feminine cursive."

Amy's brother frowned. "That's my real handwriting."

A bark of laughter escaped Ephram. "Whoops."

"Stay away from Amy." Her bother took a step closer. The buttheads moved up a step, too. "She's got a boyfriend. She tell you that?"

He felt as if he'd been smashed in the skull with a hammer. Recovering, Ephram said, "It didn't come up," as if he didn't particularly care one way or the other. A crucial guy skill. "But neither did you. We just covered the important stuff."

A string of thoughts about Amy now streamed through his mind: *She never said she had a boyfriend. But I never asked her. Being friends, that's something. But isn't it kind of weird to hang with a guy alone, like we did that day at lunch, if there's a boyfriend somewhere?*

"Nice backpack. Did you buy it at one of those fancy New York City stores?" said Amy's brother, smirking at the goons, neither of whom had managed a word. "Wonder what's in it."

It was like giving robots an order. The nearest guy grabbed Ephram's backpack, ripped open the zipper, and dumped the contents onto the dirt trail.

The guy was an idiot, but he managed to go straight for the best book in Ephram's manga collection.

"This is Ito. His stuff's way expensive," the guy holding the comic volunteered.

"What do you say we double its value?" Amy's brother asked as he took the book and began to slowly rip the book in half. Ephram considered his options. Going nuclear when the ratio was three-to-one wasn't the smart option. The comic would still be ripped. He'd get pummeled. So he watched. Hate building up inside him. Who would have thought Amy's brother would be such an—

"Bright! Stop it!"

He knew that voice. Amy. He turned and saw her standing several feet away, her brown eyes blazing, cheeks flushed.

"Bright? That's his name? Ironic." Ephram turned back to face her brother. Amy moved up beside him, making it two-to-three.

"Tell him, Amy," Bright ordered, all his attention on his sister. "Tell him why you're *really* hanging out with him."

Great, Ephram thought. *There's something else Amy didn't tell me.* He looked over at her. The blood had drained from her face. She looked guilty. One-hundred-percent guilty. *Give me a chance to explain,* she silently asked him with her brown eyes.

I asked you if you had an agenda, he silently

answered her with a look of his own. *You said no. Clearly you lied.*

All Ephram wanted was to get out of there. Bright could use the comic for a diaper if he wanted. And Amy—he had no desire to hear whatever lame explanation or apology she was silently crafting.

"Ephram, I can explain—," Amy began, just the way he knew she would.

"Forget about it," Ephram cut her off. "There's nothing to say." He turned to her brother. "Don't worry, *Bright*. I'll be staying away from your sister. For good."

He felt something rip inside his chest as he said the words. Hoping the pain didn't show on his face, he started down the hill away from them.

"By the way, dude, nice dad," Bright called after him. "I'm just curious, was he always a headcase or just since your mom bought it?"

That was it. Ephram spun around and launched himself at Bright, tackling him to the ground. He got in one good punch—solid, satisfying. Then Bright flipped him, and it was over. He was getting pummeled—stomach, kidney, face. Bright was definitely the athletic type.

"Bright, stop!" Amy yelled, as Ephram felt Bright being dragged off him. A second later, he saw Amy go up on her tiptoes and pop Bright in the eye.

Fifteen minutes later, Ephram, Bright, Amy, and

EVERWOOD

the goons were waiting outside the principal's office.

Twenty-five minutes later, Ephram was riding home with his father in silence. They pulled up in front of their house. Andy turned off the ignition, but he didn't open his door. *Here it comes,* thought Ephram. *The trapped-in-the-car conversation—a parental favorite.* The worst. Ephram was feeling claustrophobic to begin with, and being stuck in the car with his dad seemed to suck the oxygen out of the SUV completely.

"What've you got to say for yourself?" his father finally asked.

Like it was my fault, whatever happened, Ephram thought, staring out the window, concentrating on breathing normally, even though his lungs were seizing up, trying to get any air at all.

"Give it up," Ephram said. He wanted to reach for the door handle, but he didn't want to give his father the satisfaction.

"I thought you'd change, Ephram. I thought if we moved here you'd stop with the acting out," his dad said.

Acting out. Where did he come up with that one? Ephram thought. *Has he been sneaking home, watching* Dr. Phil? *He probably wouldn't give a crap except that in a town this size everyone will know that the Great Dr. Brown's kid got in a fight. How humiliating for him.*

"I got this black eye 'cause of you, dick," Ephram

muttered, kinda hoping his father would hear, kinda hoping he wouldn't. He didn't wait to find out. He got out of the car and slammed the door behind him.

Slam! His dad was out of the car and in his face. "Keep talking like that and you'll get another."

Fine. Maybe his dad needed to start thinking about the way his *own* behavior affected his precious reputation. "Want to know why I went after Bright?" Ephram moved in on his father. "He said you were crazy. And newsflash, *you are!* You quit your job. You grew this ugly-ass beard. You look like you wore your clothes to bed. You move us to Nowheresville, USA, where it's like two friggin' degrees. And for what reason? Because someone told you it was pretty! You buy an office because it smells like Mom. You don't charge your patients."

Ephram knew that he was going into forbidden territory here. This was not the kind of stuff a kid got to say to a parent. But he couldn't stop. "And if all that's not bad enough, you talk to Mom like she's still here. Yeah, I've seen you. And Delia has too. So what have I got to say for myself? *What have you got to say for yourself?*"

He didn't know what to expect. He didn't know if his dad would storm into the house and never speak to him again. Or start bawling. Or shout at him for hours, or what.

But his father just looked at him for a moment,

then said, "I can't believe you think my beard is ugly."

That's it. A lame joke. Did he hear anything I said? Ephram thought. "Mom never would have done this to us," he shouted, acid fury surging through him. "She wouldn't have gone crazy! Or moved us here!"

"Don't be so sure about that," his dad answered.

So smug, like he understood so much that Ephram never would. "I *am* sure," Ephram shot back. "*I* knew her. *You* didn't. You were never around. We all just tolerated you."

"That's pretty good. What else you got?" Andy yelled.

"I wish you'd died instead of her!" Ephram yelled. It was the truth. He'd never let himself even think it, and now he'd shouted it across the neighborhood.

"I wish I did too, you little bastard," his father spat.

It was as if the ground had fallen out from under Ephram's feet. For a second, he actually thought he was going to fall, but he recovered fast. "I hate you!" he screamed.

"I hate you right back!" his dad shouted. "Get in that house!"

But there's no way Ephram could be that close to his father. No possible way. Not right now. He grabbed his bike out of the back of the SUV. "I'm going for a ride!"

"Oh yeah?" his father demanded.

"Yeah!" Ephram yelled back.

He rode off, pedaling as hard as he could, leaving his father staring after him. Powerless. Out of the corner of his eye, Ephram noticed that their neighbor Nina Feeney had witnessed at least part of the fight. Good. She thought his dad was so wonderful. Now at least she'd gotten an eyeful of the real Andy Brown.

"At some point you're getting in this house," he heard his dad shout in the distance.

Not anytime soon, Ephram thought as he rode off, bruised and battered inside and out.

Ephram was looking forward to getting to school the next morning about as much as he had been to return home last night. Luckily, his dad knew enough to stay away from him.

Unlike Amy, who was waiting for him by the bike rack. He rolled his eyes and pedaled over to lock up his bike. "Hey," she said as soon as he stopped. He didn't answer. She didn't take the hint. "I expected you wouldn't talk to me," she said. "So I brought a peace offering. Here."

She handed him the comic books her brother and the goons had taken, including the one Bright had torn in half. Amy had neatly taped it back together. Ephram ran his thumb over the smooth piece of tape. She'd done a nice job. "Why should I talk to you, Amy?" he asked, relieved to hear his voice coming out calm and even. "So you can lie to me some more?"

"I didn't lie to you, Ephram." She glanced away, then met his gaze with what seemed like an effort. "I just . . . I didn't get a chance to tell you the whole truth, is all. I still haven't."

Ephram had made the mistake of looking at her too long. God, she was beautiful. How could he not want to stand here and listen to her say . . . anything. Lies. Truth. Whatever.

"Okay, so I know that your dad is the town's other doctor now, which, who cares, except maybe our dads," Ephram said. Dr. Abbott had been less than cordial with Dr. Brown outside the principal's office the day before.

"My grandmother, Edna, is your dad's nurse, just so you have the whole picture," Amy volunteered. "It doesn't help things, because she used to be *my* dad's nurse. Long story."

Ephram nodded, but he didn't care about that either. He forced himself to ask the big question. "Do you have a boyfriend?"

"Yes," she said firmly. No hint of hope, like, "but we're about to break up," or anything.

"I want you to meet him," Amy continued. "If you do, you'll understand."

Ephram's stomach started pumping acid at the thought. "Sure. It was on my list of things to do today. Right between picking up my dry cleaning and chopping off my hand."

But Amy was relentless. "He's in Denver," she continued. "That's three hours from here, over four by bus. If we're gonna be back by dinner, we have to leave now." She took off, assuming he'd follow her.

And he did.

Ephram ran through a couple of hundred scenarios on the bus ride. A college guy. A college professor. A drummer in a band. But he didn't even come close.

"That's him?" he asked, peering through the glass. It was a stupid question. But he repeated it anyway. "That's your boyfriend?"

"Ephram Brown, meet Colin Hart," Amy said.

Ephram continued to stare through the glass into the hospital room. A guy about his age lay on the bed, surrounded by an arsenal of life support equipment. Before Ephram could form another question, Amy began to speak.

"Colin grew up down the block from me. We did everything together. He was the first boy I ever hated, the first boy I ever hit, kissed. . . . Bright and him were best friends. They were always getting into trouble. Last July Fourth they decided to swipe Colin's father's truck and go for a joy ride."

Ephram could see where this was headed. He

wished he could stop her right here or change the ending or something. But all he could do was listen. "Colin drove," Amy went on. "There was an accident. Bright was thrown from the vehicle. He doesn't remember what happened. By the time the ambulance got there, Colin had lost consciousness. He hasn't woken up since. Every night, I've prayed for a miracle. But nothing happens."

For a moment, Ephram pictured his mother lying there in Colin's place. Not alive, not dead. How did Amy do it? How did she function? How did she show up at school every day? How did she talk and eat and smile?

"Then I read about your dad moving you all here," Amy told him, "and I realized, if anyone could help him it would be your father."

There it is, Ephram thought. *The agenda.* But he couldn't summon up any anger.

"I'm sorry if I hurt your feelings, Ephram," she said. "I was going to tell you. I just didn't know how."

I'm in love with her, Ephram realized, shocking himself. *I am completely in love with this girl.*

He watched her as she watched Colin. *And she is completely in love with that guy.*

CHAPTER 3

"You're playing," Ephram's father commented from the doorway.

Ephram glanced over and saw Delia there, too. They both had this weird expression on their faces, like they were watching a chicken playing tic-tac-toe. *Man, it hasn't been* that *long since I've touched the piano,* Ephram thought.

"I felt like it. That's all," he answered, turning away from them, continuing to play the piece he'd prepared for that last recital. But really there was a reason he felt like playing: seeing Amy with Colin. Somehow it made Ephram question whether his policy of locking away the most important thing he and his mother had together was the right thing to do.

"I'm gonna finish setting the table," Delia announced. She always was a smart kid. She knew when he wanted to be alone.

His dad, of course, didn't move. "How was your day?"

Ephram's shoulders stiffened. He felt kind of bad about yesterday's blowup. He *had* said some pretty terrible things to his father. But he was planning on just pretending the argument didn't happen, figuring that was the most painless way to go—for both of them.

"Okay," Ephram answered. "I found out I'm in love with a girl who's in love with a guy who's in a coma." He continued to play, surprised at the amount of truth that had come spilling out. "But other than that, it was pretty standard."

His dad squeezed onto the piano bench next to Ephram. He could feel the warmth of his father's body radiating into the space between them. He continued to play, conscious of every motion.

"About yesterday," his father began. "I said some things I didn't mean."

Just remembering the fight made Ephram's stomach curl into a ball. "We both did," he answered.

"Then that comment about my beard . . ."

"That I meant," Ephram said firmly, glad his father was keeping things light.

"I'm not shaving it, y'know," his dad announced, sounding like Delia in one of her stubborn moods.

"So don't," Ephram told him. "It's ugly. But it's also kinda . . ." He searched for the right word as he ran his fingers over the keys. "Distinguished."

"Distinguished? What makes you say that?"

Ephram shrugged. "I don't know. It just is."

His father seemed to have run out of questions. He just listened. And Ephram just played. Played for his mom. But for his dad, too. For Delia in the kitchen, stuck in this bizarre new life. For Amy, with her non-boyfriend. And yeah, for Colin. He played for himself, too.

"You play so well," his dad finally said. "I forgot how good you are."

Ephram continued, not ready to stop yet. "Mom used to say I have your hands." He looked over at his father, meeting his eyes for the first time since their fight.

"Okay. Give it to me," Amy said the next morning. She'd found him at his locker before first period.

"Uh, excuse me?" Ephram asked.

"Your academic update," she explained. "You've been here a week. What do you think of your classes?"

"I think they're as annoying and dull as my New York classes, just farther west," he answered. *So is this a slow, twisty lead-in to Colin and whether my dad can help him?* Ephram wondered. *Or is she going to wait for me to bring it up? Or is she going to wait a few days to bring it up so it won't seem like it's the only reason she bothers to talk to me? Or maybe she does actually talk to me for other reasons.*

45

Ephram closed his locker, and he and Amy started down the hall. *Don't think so much,* he ordered himself.

"I have to warn you," Amy said. "There's a movement to issue the new kid a nickname."

Ephram gave a low groan. "Why do I not like the direction this conversation is going?"

Amy laughed. "Ever had a nickname before?"

"Not one I'd care to repeat," he answered, moving left to make room for two girls so deep in conversation he knew they'd plow right into him if he didn't dodge them. "And just who's starting this movement anyway?"

"Me," Amy confessed. Ephram tried, unsuccessfully, to look pissed.

"Don't worry. It's an offensive tactic," Amy continued. "The way I see it, at some point, as the new kid, you'll get a nickname. These labels are *never* kind—they're either fun or mean. Most are mean."

"I know." Ephram snorted. "I have gym with Blackhead Davis."

"See what I mean?" Amy leaned a little closer, close enough that he got a whiff of the mint shampoo she used. God, she was killing him. "Now if you and I leak a few suggested nicknames, we'll have a real shot at making a fun one stick."

"You know, for the classic girl-next-door type, you have a real warped mind," he told her. And that was the perfect combo. If only he could be sure she wasn't using that warped mind of hers to manipulate him into getting what she wanted. If only he could be sure that this vibe—or whatever—he felt between them wasn't completely one-sided.

"It's something in the water here," Amy explained.

"So what's yours?" Ephram asked.

"My nickname? They call me—" She was interrupted by the bell. "They call me late for class." Amy gave him a girly wave. "See ya, Bubba."

"Bubba?" Ephram repeated, horrified.

Amy grinned. "Just testing one out." Ephram watched her until she disappeared into the crowd moving down the hallway. Then he realized he was standing there, staring, like a little girl who'd just seen Justin Timberlake. The bathroom was a few feet away, so he headed in—mostly so he wouldn't be standing there anymore—and took the closest stall. He heard some other guys come in, part of the rush between the first and second bells. If he didn't get a move on, he was going to be late. Ephram zipped up and headed for the sinks.

As he washed his hands, he saw three of the stall doors open in unison. Bright and his two bodyguards emerged. "Howdy, loser," Bright said, grinning.

Ephram turned to face them. "You guys choreographed a bathroom stall exit and *I'm* the loser?" The buttheads appeared to be puzzling over the word "choreographed," but Bright got in his face.

"I've noticed you're still getting cozy with my sis. I thought I told you once. She's spoken for." Ephram could smell the cereal on Bright's breath.

"Spoken for?" he repeated. "Hey, Bright, the fifties just called. They want their lingo back."

"When Colin finds out about you, he's gonna kick your sorry ass," Bright told him.

And we're back to Colin, Ephram thought. *We're always back to Colin.* "I figure I've got a slight advantage over him in that I'm, y'know, conscious." *Not that it was an advantage when it came to Amy.*

Bright grabbed Ephram's jacket in both fists, spun him around, and slammed him up against the closest stall. Ephram's feet dangled above the ground.

"Watch what you say, little man. One more comment like that, and Colin's not gonna be the only one in a coma," Bright threatened.

Ephram wished his feet were on the ground. It was hard to keep any dignity when your feet were kicking in the air like a little kid's. He pulled it together the best he could. "Statistically, I'm not that little. But according to every chart I've ever seen, you're still a moron."

Bright gave him a little push, grinding Ephram's back into the stall. "You may think I'm a moron, and you may be right, but when it comes to Amy,

I'm a genius. She's playing you, dude. Once she gets your daddy fixin' up Colin, she's not even gonna look at you anymore."

He abruptly let go of Ephram, and Ephram dropped to the floor, struggling to keep his balance. "You remember I said that," Bright said as he led his jock friends out of the bathroom.

Amy was all friendly in the hallway, Ephram thought. *But Bright could be right. It could all be an act. It could all be over the second she gets the Great Dr. Brown to help Colin. She did hesitate when Bright forced her to cop to it.* Ephram let out a sigh that felt like it came all the way up from his guts. *The moron could actually be right.*

Ephram was still debating Amy's level of sincerity when he sat down to dinner with Delia and their dad at Gino Chang's, Everwood's Chinese-Italian restaurant, complete with velvet paintings of Rome and paper lanterns.

"Who's up for going to Thaw Fest tomorrow?" their dad asked. He started to explain how there was a legend behind the fall heat wave, something about an early settler lost in a snowstorm. Ephram didn't bother listening. He was trying to figure out if he should attempt to have a real conversation with Amy about her motives.

A punch in the arm from Delia pulled him away from his thoughts. "You're going to the Thaw Fest, right?" she asked.

"I'd love to." Ephram turned to his father. "But only if you promise to take up surgery again and lobotomize me first."

"C'mon, Ephram. It'll be fun," his father coaxed, his eyes twinkling with a maniacal gleam. "There's gonna be hay rides, a Ferris wheel . . ."

"In what universe do hay rides and a Ferris wheel translate into fun?" Ephram shot back. He took a long gulp of his soda.

"Why don't you tell us how things are going with the Abbott girl?" his father asked.

Ephram almost dropped his glass. "Where did that come from?"

"Just curious," his dad said, acting way too innocent.

"Well, don't be," Ephram told him.

His dad smiled. Usually he'd be pissed if Ephram told him to mind his own business. But he was smiling. Not good. "They must be going pretty well," his father commented, "'cause Amy's walking over here."

Oh no. Not here. Not with my dad and Delia, Ephram thought.

"Hey, Bubba," Amy said when she reached them.

His father's smile got even wider, if that was possible. "Uh, Dad, you remember Amy," Ephram muttered.

His father nodded. "Hey there, Amy."

So far, so good, Ephram reassured himself. His father hadn't embarrassed him yet.

"What's your name?" Amy asked Delia.

Okay, would have been good to do that introduction. But no biggie, Ephram decided.

"I'm Delia," his little sister answered. "You're pretty."

And I'm blushing, Ephram realized, feeling the heat flood into his face. *Why did Delia have to go there?*

Luckily Andy's cell phone rang before Delia had a chance to embarrass him further.

"Excuse me, everyone," his father said. He stood up and headed for a quieter section of the restaurant.

"Just here with your dad, huh?" Ephram asked, partly to keep Delia quiet.

"Yeah. How'd you know?" Amy said.

Ephram glanced over at Dr. Abbott. He was waving both arms, signaling wildly for Amy to return to him. "He's kinda hard to miss," Ephram answered.

"Friday nights are father-daughter nights," Amy explained, her face illuminated in the soft glow of one of the Chinese lanterns. "We grab a bite to eat and go home and watch something he's taped off Turner Classics."

Ephram couldn't keep the smirk off his face. "Sounds bitchin'."

Amy shot a fast look over her shoulder at her

dad, her mouth curling up in an affectionate smile. "I know it's hard to believe, but he's kinda cool when no one's looking." She shot another glance at her father. "I better get back before he combusts. I just wanted to say hi. See ya."

"Later." For the second time that day, Ephram found himself watching Amy walk away from him, unable to decide how much he could trust her.

"Is she your girlfriend?"

Ephram jerked his head away from Amy toward his sister. Delia grinned at him like a little demon. "No, she's not my girlfriend," he told her.

Delia's grin stretched wider than Ephram would have thought possible. "But you *want* her to be."

"You're *this* close to knowing pain in a form you've never known before," Ephram warned her in a whisper as their dad came back to the table.

"That was my patient from the other night," their father announced. He put his cell back in his pocket. "I've got to get out to her place. It's an emergency."

"But we just ordered," Ephram protested. And something clicked in his head. Except for the beard, his dad could have been the New York Dr. Brown. The guy that was too important to show up for recitals or birthdays, forget about a Friday-night dinner with his kids.

"I should be back by the time you finish. If I'm not, here's some money and my phone to call a cab.

Have them take you home." He dumped the cell and cash in front of Ephram's plate. "Can you do that, Ephram?"

"Sure thing, Pops," Ephram answered, voice flat. *This was our life,* he silently added. *Mom and me and Delia. Delia was just too little to notice with Mom around to pick up the slack.*

"So, Delia, from the appetizers, are you liking the Italian or the Chinese better?" Ephram asked. That's what his mother would do. She'd try to keep Delia from realizing that she'd just been abandoned . . . again.

Ephram kept Delia talking straight through dessert—tiramisu and green tea ice cream. It was exhausting, but he did it. Then he paid the bill with his dad's cash, left a big tip—the Great Dr. Brown could afford it—and headed outside. He took his father's cell out of his pocket.

"Can I call?" Delia asked.

"Sure," Ephram told her. "First you have to call information and ask for a cab company. Say the number out loud to me when you get it. I'll help you remember it."

Ephram stared up at the night sky as Delia punched in 411 and asked for Everwood information. The stars were so bright here. He was still getting used to it. In Manhattan the lights of the buildings made it hard to see anything. Here you could even see the milky way. And the smells. He hadn't smelled urine-soaked denim cooked over a hot subway grate since he moved to Everwood. Not that that was a bad thing. But the smell was New York in a way that—

"Five five five four seven two two," Delia repeated. "Thanks." She hung up the cell. "There's only one cab in Everwood."

"Figures," Ephram muttered. In New York, he could just step off the curb, hold up his hand, and they'd be on their way. "You want to call it?"

Delia was already pushing the buttons. "It's ringing," she said. "It's ringing and ringing."

"Are you sure you dialed it right?" Ephram asked.

Delia hung up, then showed him the last number dialed. 555-4722. Ephram dialed 411. "I got it right," Delia protested.

"I just want to double check," Ephram said. He got the same information Delia did—one taxi service in Everwood: 555-4722, The Sam Randolph Cab Company. "Is there a number for Sam Randolph?" he asked.

Ephram hung up and dialed the second number he'd gotten. Not that it did him much good. He reached a message machine that said: "Hey, you've reached Sam Randolph. If you're looking for a cab ride, you're out of luck. This is my night off."

"Not working tonight," Ephram yelled into the phone. "It took me twenty minutes to track this number down and no cab tonight?" He forced himself to hang up and control his hissy fit, so as not to freak Delia out.

"Stranded?" a sympathetic voice asked.

Amy. Of course Amy had to see him behaving like an idiot. Ephram turned to face her. "Trying to get a cab," he answered. "Turns out there's only one cabbie in town and he's taken the night off."

"Mr. Randolph. He doesn't work Friday nights, 'cause he calls the bingo numbers at the Catholic church," Amy explained.

Delia moved a little closer to Ephram. He gave her baseball cap a friendly tug, trying to signal that everything was going to be okay. He just hadn't figured out exactly how yet.

"This really is the town that time forgot," Ephram told Amy.

"We can take you home. Right, Daddy?" Amy asked.

"Of course we can," Dr. Abbott said, his eyes flicking to Delia. He led the way over to the car and held the front door open for Ephram. It was very clear he didn't want Ephram sitting in the backseat with his daughter. Ephram climbed in. Amy and Delia got in the back.

Ephram knew Everwood was a small town. A very small town. But Dr. Abbott must have been sending out some kind of biotoxins in Ephram's direction, because it felt as if it took at least three solid hours to get from Gino Chang's to their house.

The payoff came when Ephram got out of the car and Amy climbed out to move into the front seat. "The Thaw Festival's tomorrow," she told Ephram as he stood on the sidewalk. "I was wondering if you were going."

"Ephram!" Delia called from the front porch.

"Just a second, Delia," Ephram answered, without looking away from Amy. "I was thinking about it. I hear there are hay rides and a Ferris wheel."

"But did you know there's also a horseshoe throwing competition?" Amy asked, mouth twitching as she tried to keep a straight face.

"Ephram!" Delia called again.

"I said just a second," Ephram called back. He shook his head. "Little sisters."

"Go easy. I am one, remember," she replied.

"Yeah, I'll be at the festival . . . of the . . . thaw." *Smooth, Ephram. Very smooth,* he thought. "That didn't quite come out right," he admitted, stating the obvious.

Amy laughed a little. "Two o'clock by the Melting Man."

"What's a Melting Man?" Ephram asked.

"You'll have to wait and see," Amy answered. And it sounded to Ephram like she was flirting—a little. Or was this all part of her plan to get him to ask his dad to help Colin? Looking at Amy right now, it was hard to care.

Beeeep! Dr. Abbott leaned on the horn.

Amy gave Ephram one last smile and ducked back into the car, shutting the door behind her with a quiet click.

Ephram turned to face Delia. "What? What was so important?"

"We're locked out," she announced, arms crossed over her chest.

Ephram looked back at the street. The Abbotts' car was gone. *Crap,* he thought.

And that wasn't his last serving of crap for the night. He sliced his hand breaking into his own house. Then he had to sit up with Delia after she had one of her monster nightmares.

But there was one thing Ephram knew for sure: He was going to spread the crap around. So he made himself comfortable on the couch and waited. He didn't care if his dad rolled in at 4 A.M. Ephram would be right there to greet him.

Finally Ephram heard the back door open. "Where have you been?" he demanded as his father stepped into the living room.

"I was stuck at the Dudleys. What's the matter? Is everything okay?" his dad replied, managing to actually sound concerned.

"No. Everything's not okay," Ephram answered. "Your daughter had a nightmare tonight."

His dad frowned. "How is she now?"

"She's fine. I got her back to sleep about thirty minutes ago," Ephram said.

"It was that movie, wasn't it? *Willy Wonka*?" his dad asked. "I should have made sure she didn't watch it."

Typical. His father was looking for one little thing that he could fix. "For a guy who was once cited by *US News & World Report* as one of the greatest minds in America, it amazes me sometimes how clueless you are. You really think this is about a movie?"

His dad tilted back his head for a long moment, staring up at the ceiling, then he looked at Ephram. "Why don't you enlighten me, Ephram, as to what it *is* about? Because that's what I need tonight, another lecture from my fifteen-year-old son."

Ephram sprang to his feet. He'd heard his father say almost the same words before. But not to him. "Don't talk to me the way you used to talk to Mom. I'm not your wife!"

"What the hell does that mean?" his father demanded, his voice razor-sharp.

"You think I want to be having this conversation with you?" Ephram yelled. "I don't. I didn't marry you. I never agreed to pick up the slack."

"Look. I apologize that I wasn't here to take care of Delia. But I was treating a ten-year-old boy who couldn't breathe—"

Of course, Ephram thought. *Of course that's what's going to come spewing out of your mouth.*

You're never going to get it. He threw up his hands. "Well, you win. Boys who can't breathe trump little girls with nightmares."

"In my profession, they do," Andy answered.

"You mean the medical profession or the crappy father one?"

"That's enough," his dad bellowed. "As of this second, you and that mouth of yours are gonna start showing me some respect or—"

"Or what?" Ephram challenged. He hated it when his father pulled out the "respect me because I gave you life" card. That's about all his dad had ever done in terms of being a parent.

Ephram and his dad locked eyes. He could see the fury burning in his father. *Come on, hit me,* Ephram thought. *Prove once and for all that you really don't care about me or Delia, or anything but yourself and being the Great Dr. Brown.*

"What's with your hand?" his dad asked, surprising Ephram.

Ephram held it up, realizing his first-aid job kind of sucked. "It's tonight's punchline. I sliced it trying to pry open a window to this place, which happened after Delia and I couldn't get a cab home, which happened after you left us at dinner, alone for the second night this week."

"Lemme take a look at it."

"It's fine."

"I said, lemme see." His dad reached for him.

Ephram jerked his hand away. He wasn't going to let his father doctor his way out of this one with a few stitches or whatever. "Don't touch me," he spat.

Andy froze, and Ephram noticed how tired he looked. Tired and . . . human. "The Great Dr. Brown," he said quietly. "That's what Mom and I used to call you. You always thought it was endearing. But it wasn't. It was our private joke. 'When's the Great Dr. Brown coming home for dinner?' 'Think the Great Dr. Brown will be here this weekend?'"

Ephram paused. He could see his dad was listening. So he went on. "Don't you see? You're still that guy. It doesn't matter if it's the Dudleys on Forest Lane like tonight, or some rich lady on Park Avenue. They'll always come first. The only difference is, this time Mom's not here to cover for you. At least I got her. Who does Delia get?"

His dad didn't answer. Maybe he couldn't. But maybe he was thinking about it. That was all Ephram could do. He walked past his father and up the stairs, feeling as if he had bags of cement strapped to each foot.

The next day, Ephram rushed toward the Melting Man as if his life depended on it. A day without family. A day *with* Amy. Total paradise.

He slowed down to a respectable speed when he

saw that she was already there waiting for him. "Hey," he said when he reached her. He didn't want to sound as if she were the only good thing in his universe.

"There you are." Amy took his arm and turned him toward an ice sculpture that was more of an ice blob with a hat and a few pieces of clothing. "Ephram Brown, the Melting Man. The Melting Man, Ephram Brown."

"He's oddly quiet," Ephram commented, half-surprised he could say anything with Amy touching him.

"He's not having the best day," Amy commented. "I think it might be his last."

Ephram scanned the crowd. They were all staring at the Melting Man like they were watching a golf tournament or something. It was that kind of hushed silence. "Everyone just watches him melt, huh?"

"It's a contest," Amy explained. "You bet when the hat's gonna hit the ground. Mr. Lawrence over there's won three years in a row."

Ephram checked out Mr. Lawrence, who wore a smug expression that said he knew he was going to win again. "I think it's safe to say we've got a few hours yet," Ephram said.

"Here's the deal. My dad agreed I could hang with you today on one condition." Amy scrunched up her nose.

"Yeah. What's that?" If he could still be with her it couldn't be too awful.

Bright stepped up, stuffing his face with cotton candy. "How goes it, bone-lick?"

"Bright has to hang with us," Amy confessed.

Ephram rolled his eyes. "No offense, but he's really my least favorite thing about you."

"Yeah?" Bright pulled a piece of cotton candy off his cheek and stuck it in his mouth. "Well *you're* my least favorite thing about *you*."

Ephram shook his head. "Dude, you gotta work on the insults."

Bright just grinned. Why shouldn't the big moose grin? He had Ephram exactly where he wanted him. He squeezed in between Ephram and Amy and wrapped an arm around each of them. "I wonder what we should hit first? Face painting? Or perhaps the silent auction?"

"Do you have that thing where you toss ping-pong balls in goldfish bowls? 'Cause I would dearly love to win me a goldfish," Ephram answered, trapped under Bright's beefy arm.

"Sure do," Bright said. He towed Amy and Ephram over to the booth, where Ephram failed to win a goldfish.

"Ferris wheel next," Amy announced.

Ephram gazed up at it. Pretty high. Pretty decrepit looking. The only good thing was that Bright let him and Amy into one of the cars by themselves. As the car soared up, Ephram's stomach plunged down. And he could hear something metallic groaning. That couldn't be good.

"I'm shocked Bright didn't shove himself in here with us," Ephram said, hoping to distract Amy from the look of terror he was sure was on his face.

"I knew he wouldn't go near this thing. He's deathly afraid of heights," Amy answered.

The car jerked to a stop at the very top of the wheel. Ephram grabbed the metal safety bar with both hands, then immediately released it when he realized what he'd done.

"Don't worry," Amy said. "It's part of the ride."

Ephram snorted. "So what do people do up here? Apart from wait for an early demise?"

Amy shot him a *duh* look. A second later, Ephram caught a glimpse of the couple in the car below them making out. "And ask dumb questions," he added quickly.

Is that why Amy brought me on this thing? he thought. *'Cause I'd brave a lot worse to kiss her. I'd—*

"I brought you up here to tell you something," Amy said.

Oh.

"Grover," she continued.

"Grover?" he repeated.

"It's my nickname. I always loved Grover as a kid. I know, with most girls it's all Winnie the

63

Pooh or Hello Kitty or occasionally Strawberry Shortcake. But with me, life was about a little blue Muppet named Grover."

Ephram nodded, trying to get his bearings, trying to forget that other people were making out. "Grover was a very underrated Muppet."

Amy looked at him like he'd just said something wonderfully intelligent. "Colin and Bright would torment me for hours by stealing my Grover doll and hiding him. Then one day, Colin refused to give me the doll back unless I kissed him first—Colin that is, not Grover, whom I had kissed many times."

I so don't want to hear this, Ephram thought. *When is this contraption going to start moving again?*

"So I closed my eyes," Amy continued, her voice soft with memory, "and Colin closed his, we both leaned forward . . . and I kicked him right in the nuts—Colin that is, not Grover, who didn't have nuts. At least none that I was aware of."

Ephram smiled, but his mind was filled with an image of Colin lying in that hospital bed, surrounded by all those machines keeping him alive.

"Anyway, Colin screamed and doubled over. My parents raced into the room," Amy went on. "And when they asked what happened, Colin wouldn't tell them. All he would say was that Grover did it. And suddenly, somehow, I'd developed my first crush—on Colin that is, not Grover."

When she talks about him, she looks even more beautiful, Ephram thought, studying Amy's face. She didn't speak for a long moment. Neither did he. But Ephram was pretty sure they were both thinking about the same thing. Not about how romantic it would be to kiss on the very top of the Ferris wheel, though that did cross his mind, but about Colin. It always came back to Colin.

"I know we haven't talked about it since that trip to Denver," Amy finally began.

Ephram didn't make her say it. "You want me to ask my dad to help Colin."

"If you could just talk to him. There's probably nothing he can do, but—"

Ephram cut her off again. "Sure, Amy. Yeah. I'll ask him."

The Ferris wheel jerked forward. And Ephram felt his heart break.

CHAPTER 4

When Ephram climbed off the Ferris wheel, the ground felt like it was trembling beneath his feet. He could come up with some excuse, like the contrast between the motion of the wheel and the stillness of the ground, but it would be bull. Even in the most romantic setting—like something out of a freakin' movie—Amy was thinking of Colin.

Their chaperone stepped right up to them. If Amy's father knew what really went on in his daughter's head, he'd know there was no need to have Bright tagging along. The thought of Colin was all the chaperone Amy needed.

"There's something you've gotta see," Bright said, not sounding quite as jovial as he had before. Maybe even *watching* the Ferris wheel gave him the wiggin's. Ephram and Amy followed him past the horseshoe toss and the pink lemonade stand.

Ephram could see a small crowd gathered around—
His father.

Ephram pushed his way closer, hardly aware
that Amy stayed by his side. His eyes were locked
on his dad, whose eyes were fastened on someone
who wasn't there. And Andy was having a conversation with that someone.

"Fine isn't great," his dad said, sounding resigned.
Then he was silent, listening.

"What do you want me to say?" he finally asked,
with a catch in his voice. Ephram's own throat
closed up. He knew who his father was talking to.
Mom.

Ephram's dad listened again. The crowd was
hushed, just like they had been watching the
Melting Man. But the mood was tense, most of
the faces deathly serious.

"Not to you," his father said. "Just to . . . this."
Ephram could hardly stand to watch. Because it
was humiliating to be standing there, the son of a
freak. But also because it was so personal, so private, a moment that should have been between his
parents alone. Ephram knew that was nuts, but
that's how it felt—at least to him.

"Talking to you this way," his dad continued, off
in his own world, "it's just not very healthy. In fact,
it sorta borders on psychotic." His father raised his
eyebrows in response to something only he could
hear. "You do? And you're okay with it?"

It might be worth being crazy to really see her again, Ephram thought suddenly. *To talk to her.* Then he spotted Delia in the crowd. What was this doing to his little sister? How freaked was she? Her brown eyes were huge, her face solemn. But she was holding it together.

"This is kind of a raw deal, isn't it?" his father asked.

It sure the hell is, Ephram silently answered him. He wondered if he should go up to his dad, try to bring him out of it. Would that make it worse?

"I don't get it," his dad said, still unaware of the crowd—Nina and her little boy; Delia's bus driver, Mr. Irv, who was holding hands with his wife, Edna; Dr. Abbott; the buttheads from school.

Ephram's father cocked his head as he listened to the response. "Know who?" he asked. "What are you—"

A little kid's balloon popped. The sound was like a gunshot in the funeral-like silence. And Ephram saw his father being jerked back into the real world, the world without Julia Brown. Alone in the center of the crowd, his dad stared into the faces of all the people around him, seeing them for the first time.

Before Ephram could move—before he could decide if he *wanted* to move toward his father— Delia stepped up to their dad. Although she whispered, her words were easy to hear, "Let's go home." She held out her hand. And Andy took it.

It's so easy for her, Ephram thought as he joined his dad and sister and walked away from the crowd. *So easy to . . . to love him. Step up, no matter what.* Maybe partly because she didn't have the years of experience Ephram had with the Great Dr. Brown. But it wasn't just that. She was a brave little kid. Braver than he was, in some ways.

They made their way to the parking lot and climbed into the SUV. It was like a decompression tank for them. The time they spent in it during the ride home gave them time to come up from the strange dark waters of what had happened at the festival to something like a normal environment.

"So," their father said after they pulled into their own driveway. "What did everyone think of the festival?"

"That's not funny," Ephram said. He was going to get so much crap at school over this. And maybe . . . maybe there were more than a few screws loose in his dad's head. Enough to make him fall apart completely.

"It was a little funny," his father answered.

Ephram laughed—it just came bubbling out of him. His dad laughed too. Then Delia laughed because they were laughing. *First time we've all laughed together since Mom died,* Ephram realized. *And it's 'cause Dad was having a conversation with her ghost in front of the whole town.*

The thought made him laugh harder, and the laughter shook every muscle in his body loose, even muscles he hadn't realized were tense. He hadn't realized it was possible to clench your toes.

"Does anyone here even know what a Thaw Festival is, 'cause I just went to one, and I'm still not sure," Ephram asked, still snorting with laughter. His question started up a fresh round of giggles, even though he hadn't said anything that funny. Then Delia handed their dad a note.

"What's this?" he asked.

"A note from school. I'm in big trouble. Ha, ha, ha, ha"—Delia opened her door—"see you inside," she said then bolted.

"You know anything about this?" his dad asked, suddenly serious again.

They both stared after Delia. Ephram shook his head and said, "She's crafty, that one. You have to give her that." Neither Ephram nor his dad made a move to leave the SUV. It was safe in there. Not quite the real world. But not quite la-la land either.

"I see her too, sometimes," Ephram admitted. "Mom. Not like you do. I don't talk to her or anything. It's like I feel her . . . y'know, with us." He'd been talking directly to the dashboard, but now he looked over at his father. And his dad was *there*, one-hundred-percent focused on Ephram. "When we're eating dinner, or when there's a song playing on the radio that she used to like. I know she's there."

His father nodded. He hesitated a moment, then he began to speak. "Ephram, I wish I could tell you that everything was gonna be okay. I know that's what I'm supposed to say. The truth is, I don't know what's gonna happen to us."

It was a scary thing to hear his father say. The Great Dr. Brown never admitted he didn't know everything—even when he was most clueless. But the Great Dr. Brown wasn't in the car right now. It was just Ephram's dad.

"What I do know is that all we have now is each other," his father continued. "And I need your help. I need your help raising your sister. I can't do it alone." He paused again, then he said, "She gets *us*."

So he was listening to me the other night, Ephram realized, hearing the answer to the question he'd asked his father in round ninety-nine of their ongoing battle. *That's something.*

As expected, when he showed up at school on Monday, Ephram got teased about his dad. And he didn't care all that much. After the conversation in the SUV, Ephram wasn't afraid that his father was going to drift off into some happy daydream place and never come back. He was going to be there for Ephram and Delia. He wasn't nuts. End of story.

And the one person at school he actually cared about, Amy, treated him the same as always. Monday at lunch she had a new nickname to run by him: Broody. He nixed it.

Tuesday Ephram suggested Psycho Spawn. Amy vetoed, and told him he wasn't allowed to nickname himself. She insisted she only needed a little more time to think.

On Friday, she spotted him in the library and greeted him with "How's it going there, Ham?"

"Ham?" Ephram repeated.

"It's your new nickname," she said firmly. "Welcome to it."

"My nickname is a deli item?" he asked, basking in the Amy glow.

Amy smiled at him, the kind of smile that separated the two of them into a little section of the school that no one could enter. A private place in the middle of a crowd. "That's what everyone will think," Amy agreed. "But we'll know it's really short for this. . . ." She rummaged around among the books she had stacked on the library table, and pulled out a worn paperback copy of *Hamlet*. Ephram stared at it. "See. You look like him." Amy tapped the guy on the cover.

"That does not look like me," Ephram protested. *It looks like Michel Bolton before the haircut,* he thought.

"No, no. You can't deny it. Everwood finally has

72

its own Dark Prince. Wanna get some lunch?" she asked.

And it hit him. Ephram didn't know if anyone else would have seen it. But he did. And he should have sooner. Because he was betting it had been there all week. The flicker of anxiety that tightened Amy's voice. The tension that had her shoulders riding just a tiny bit higher.

The question in her eyes.

He'd spent all week yammering about nick-names, enjoying his Amy buzz, and inside she was going nuts. "Lunch, sure," Ephram answered. "But before we go in, we have to talk."

"You asked your father, didn't you?" Amy asked, her voice coming out slightly higher than normal.

Ephram nodded. It wasn't true, but he nodded anyway.

He hadn't come up with some big plan to lie to her. But if she knew there was definitely no chance for Colin—and there wasn't really, was there?— then he and Amy could keep . . . being he and Amy.

Her eyes began to dart back and forth—the tiniest of motions—as she studied his expression for an indication of what he was going to say next.

"He said no. . . .You can't really begrudge the guy. He's trying to get out of the brain business. Start a new life." The words came vomiting up out of him. Complete lies.

"It was silly for me to ask in the first place," Amy

said quickly. "I don't know what I was thinking."

"I'm sorry, Amy," Ephram told her.

She turned her face away from him, shielding whatever she was feeling from his eyes. *Is a part of her relieved?* Ephram wondered. *Is she hating me right now for being the messenger? The lying messenger,* he couldn't help adding. But his father probably wouldn't have been able to do anything. Colin had been in a coma for months.

"Still wanna grab some lunch?" Ephram asked.

"You know, I'm just gonna hang here and go over some notes before class," Amy answered a little too casually. Her shoulders had ratcheted up even higher, and her arms were wrapped low over her belly, like she'd just taken a blow to the gut. "I'll see you later."

Ephram didn't want to leave. But it was so clearly what she wanted that he did. When he passed the library's big windows, he couldn't stop himself from looking in to check on her. Amy was turned away from him, but it was clear from the way her shoulders were shaking that she was crying.

What did I do? he thought as he looked at her. *What did I just do?*

As the days passed, Amy pretended everything was fine. And Ephram let her. Sometimes he tried to pretend too—that he hadn't lied to her, that he didn't realize how incredibly important his father's help was to Amy, that she might possibly ever get over Colin.

He wasn't as good at pretending as she was, so he started avoiding her. Just a little. Just as much as he could bear.

In the mornings he sought out Wendell instead of Amy. Wendell was the closest thing Ephram had found to a friend at school—which wasn't very close. Possibly because Wendell spent so much time brokering favors between students and scooping up bonuses for himself that he didn't actually have time for friendship.

One day Ephram stopped at Wendell's locker, which had a pinecone, a twig, and a couple of leaves hanging from it. "Cool," Wendell said, coming up behind him. "An abundance of riches."

"Why do you have pieces of nature hanging on your locker?" Ephram looked around and noticed that Wendell's locker wasn't the only one sprouting. "And why aren't you alone in this?"

"Are you aware of the Fall Dance that's coming up?" Wendell asked.

"I've seen posters," Ephram answered.

"Observant. I like it." Wendell fingered one of the leaves appreciatively. "Well, the Fall Dance is special in that it's one of those dances where the girls ask the boys. And the *way* they ask us is sort of a tradition around here."

Ephram raised an eyebrow. "They forage through the woods and decorate your locker with bark?"

"Close. It's the Fall Dance, see, so first they have to find something that *falls* from trees," Wendell explained. "Pinecones, leaves, overly ripened fruit."

Unbelievable, Ephram thought. "When you guys come up with these traditions, are you still high on the crack, or are you just coming down?"

Wendell ignored Ephram, as usual. "Once the girls have chosen an item, they tie a ribbon around it, sign their names to it, and place it on your locker as a way of formally inviting you." Wendell ran his finger down the twig. "Check your locker?"

"That's okay. I think I'll pass."

"Be positive, my man." Wendell clapped him on the shoulder and strolled off. Ephram held out for about three seconds, then he walked quickly down the hall, heading for his own locker. When he turned the corner, his locker came into sight. A single pinecone hung from the door.

Ephram froze for a second. Yeah, he'd rushed over there, but he hadn't been expecting anything. Not really. In three long strides, he was at his locker. He grabbed the pinecone and ripped it free. His fingers trembled as he read the note: *To—Ephram. From—Amy.*

He had to see her. Had to. Right now.

Ephram tracked Amy down in the library. Unfortunately she was studying with Kayla, a girl who consistently treated Ephram like dirt. Screw it. He didn't want to wait. He walked straight over, the pinecone still in his hand.

"Hey, Ephram. What's up?" Amy asked.

"Nothing. I, uh . . ." How much did he wish Kayla wasn't there? "I wanted to ask you—"

"FYI, only girls can give the pinecones," Kayla announced, interrupting. "It's, like, a rule."

"Yeah, I'm aware of that, Kayla," Ephram informed her. "Someone left this for me. On my locker."

"Who?" Amy asked.

Who? That one explained everything. "Oh . . . uh," Ephram stammered. *Say something. Cover,* he ordered himself.

Too late. Cackles of laughter erupted. It didn't take long to find the source. Bright and the buttheads.

"Oh, no, Ephram," Amy exclaimed. "Did you think it was me?"

"No," Ephram said, much, much too late. "But I just wanted to confirm." He didn't give her a chance to say anything else. He had to get out of there. But he took the time to pause at Bright's table. "I guess I overestimated you. I thought you'd at least come up with a new way of messing with me."

"Why bother?" Bright asked. "You keep falling for the same old trick." He laughed as Ephram stormed toward the exit. "What a tool," Bright called after him.

As soon as Ephram reached the hallway, he had to stop. His lungs didn't feel like they were working. He couldn't pull in a full breath. Suddenly Amy was there, and he didn't want to see her.

"I apologize for my brother," Amy said. "I know he's a jerk sometimes—"

"Try all the time," Ephram shot back, managing to control his breathing so he didn't look like he was having an asthma attack.

"If it makes you feel any better, Ephram, I didn't ask you to the dance because I'm not asking anyone," Amy explained, her brown eyes brimming with sincerity. "I'm not even going myself."

"Fine. Whatever," Ephram said. *Just go away,* he silently begged her. *I can't deal with you right now.*

"It just feels weird. Last year I asked Colin and—"

He couldn't stand to hear another long, sweet story about Colin. It would break him. And he couldn't allow that. Not in the middle of freakin' County High School.

"I said *fine,*" Ephram interrupted, the words coming out more harshly than he meant them to. "I don't need to hear about your stupid boyfriend every other minute. I get it. I *get* it."

Ephram had time to see Amy's face go pale before he looked away and walked out.

She didn't call to him. He didn't expect her to. He didn't *want* her to.

Ephram was sure his life couldn't possibly get any worse. Then the next night at dinner, his father announced that he and Dr. Abbott were planning to give a sex education talk at Ephram's school. And his dad actually seemed baffled that Ephram had a problem with that. Clueless. The Clueless Dr. Brown.

The next morning, Ephram locked up his bike and headed toward the school, wondering who would be the first to give him hell about the sex assembly. He spotted Amy walking toward the main building. She didn't seem too eager to get there either. Why would she? Her dad was giving the sex talk too.

Automatically, Ephram picked up his pace so he'd catch up to her. But after what he'd said about Colin, he was sure she didn't want him within a hundred feet of her. He slowed down. She slowed down a little too. So maybe . . .

Ephram swallowed hard. "Hey," he called.

Amy paused and turned toward him. "Are we back to greeting each other?" she asked, without smiling. "I wasn't sure."

"I am if you are," Ephram answered.

"I was never mad at you, Ephram," Amy said.

How was that possible? "Well, you should be,"

he told her. "I said some dumb things the other day." *The understatement of the century,* he thought. "I'm sorry."

Amy looked up and studied the sky for a second, as if she were searching for any answer up there. Then she looked at him and said, "Why don't we stop with all the back and forth apologies and assume that we're both, like, sorry forever. Deal?"

Ephram felt like his bones had turned liquid with relief. "Yeah, sure. Deal."

They started walking again—slowly. "Can you believe our dads are coming to school today?" Amy asked. "It must be the end of the world or something."

"It's bad enough I have to see him every morning and night. Afternoons are my time off, you know?" Ephram commented, feeling totally in sync with her.

"I know what you mean. I kind of hate both my parents these days," Amy said.

"Really? You seem like such the well-adjusted family unit."

"Oh, sure," Amy answered sarcastically. "My father has OCD, my brother has ADD, and my mother is just plain crazy."

"And what are you?"

It was a real question, and Amy treated it that way. She stopped and thought about it, then said, "I'm tired."

The way she said it, it was clear she didn't mean that she had stayed up too late last night. It was more like she was soul tired. "Amy? Are you okay?" Ephram asked, hoping she would keep being honest with him.

"No, I'm not," she told him. "And this dance is just making me feel worse. My mom keeps bugging me about it. . . . It's like nobody understands why this is hard for me." She pulled in a deep, shuddering breath. "I'm sorry. I know you don't want—"

"We're both already sorry forever, remember?" Ephram said, wishing he could do something for her besides just *talk*.

"I wanted to ask him, you know? Like last year. I just want to feel normal again—just for one second—instead of how I feel now." They reached the entrance to the school, and Amy leaned against the wall, as if she was too exhausted to go any farther.

Looking at her, Ephram realized there was a way he could help Amy. It would be torturous for him, however. "If that's what you want to do, then you should do it," he told her, with effort.

Her brows drew together. "What are you talking about?"

"Ask Colin . . . to the dance." He said the words she had once said to him. "He's three hours from here. Four by bus. If we're gonna be back by dinner, we have to leave now."

Amy pushed herself away from the wall. "Ephram . . ."

"I would give anything to be able to talk to my mom again," he explained. "It wouldn't even matter to me if she could answer. I'd just be happy to see her." He tried to imagine what that would be like. To see his mom's face. Sometimes it was hard to bring it up in his mind. "You can still see him, Amy. You can still ask him."

A little more than four and a half hours later, Ephram again found himself sitting outside Colin's hospital room. Waiting for Amy. Listening as she told Colin all about the Fall Dance.

"Kim Einhorn asked David Lee, which nobody thought she'd ever have the nerve to do. I swear, ever since she got her braces off, she's like this totally new person. And he said yes, which was so cool. Oh, and the decorating committee is going all out this year. Ali's mom wants to turn the gym into a magical forest. I know it sounds bizarre, but Ali says her mom is practically a professional with that stuff, so it should look amazing."

There was a pause in Amy's endless rush of words. When she began to speak again, her voice was softer. The voice a girlfriend only uses with her boyfriend. It slashed Ephram up inside to hear that voice, but he didn't move. He was going to be right there when Amy was done. She was gonna need him.

"I guess now the only thing that's missing is you and me," Amy told Colin. "Which is why I'm here. I know this is last minute and everything, but I was wondering . . . would you go to the dance with me?"

Ephram leaned forward, body tense, praying for Amy to get her *yes*.

But the only response was the steady beeping of Colin's life-support machines.

"Just open your eyes, Colin. Please," Amy begged, voice breaking.

Beep. Beep. Beep. Beep.

Ephram watched Amy attack her burger. She went after the thing with a vengeance. "Slow down," he told her. "You don't have to inhale it. We have plenty of time before the bus back to Everwood."

"I'm so starving. I didn't even realize," Amy said.

I wonder when's the last time she really ate. Or slept. Or actually had fun, Ephram thought, glad she was at least getting some food down now. She looked better, too, he realized. Shoulders down. Not so . . . twisted up in general.

Amy swallowed the bite of burger, washing it down with some of her strawberry milkshake. "Thanks for coming with me, Ephram," she said.

"It's cool. I was hungry too." He rattled the ice around in his glass of Cherry Coke.

"No. I mean thanks for coming all the way here. To Denver and the hospital and everything," Amy clarified. "It means a lot to me."

Ephram struggled to continue meeting Amy's gaze. He suddenly felt like scum. There was so much more he could have done for Amy, like ask his dad to help Colin. *Not that it would have done any good,* Ephram told himself. *I mean, Colin's doctors would have told his parents if there was any kind of chance at all. Right?*

Right. Except for one little thing. Not one of Colin's doctors was the Great Dr. Brown, miracle worker. Ephram always left out that fact when he tried to convince himself that nothing could be done for Colin.

"Yeah, well . . . I didn't want to be in school today anyway." Ephram took a slug of his soda. "What with my dad showing up as porn king and all."

Amy shook her head. "I'm sure it wasn't as bad as you think."

"Maybe not for you," Ephram answered. "But for me? I can't even imagine the damage control I'm gonna have to do because of this."

"What do you mean?" Amy took another giant bite of her burger. Ephram had to use two napkins to keep the mustard that came flooding out the burger's other side from running all the way down her arm.

"C'mon," he said, balling up the napkins. "Like our classmates need any more ammunition to use against me. I now have to be known as Boner Boy?"

Amy studied him, her head tilted to the side. "Was it this bad for you in New York?"

"You mean was I this big of a geek back home, too?" He scratched the corner of his eyebrow.

"I didn't mean it like that."

"It's okay," Ephram reassured her. A memory hit him, and he started telling her about it, just assuming she'd want to hear. "I almost went to one dance at my old school. The winter semiformal. I asked Catherine Addams to go. She wasn't the most popular girl in school, but she was the prettiest. She had this kind of punky Gwen Stefani look going on, which not too many girls in high school can pull off. But she did."

Ephram paused, trying to picture Amy punked out. He didn't think she could pull off Gwen Stefani, but she was way more beautiful than Gwen or Catherine.

"Anyway," he went on, "my friends dared me to ask her, and she actually said yes. Which was like, shock. So, day of the dance, my mom is all excited. She's showing me how to pin a corsage on a girl. I swear, I must've stuck my mom with that pin like five times, but she never said anything."

It feels good to talk about her, Ephram realized.

He and his dad and Delia never just told stories about his mom. And Amy seemed totally into it, like she could listen to a hundred stories and not get sick of them.

"Six o'clock, Catherine calls," Ephram told her. "She's sick. She can't go. Now I can't tell my mom this, because she's so happy. And I don't want her to find out what a loser her son is. So I get all dressed up in my suit, take the corsage, and walk out the door, like I'm gonna go pick up Catherine. Except, of course, I don't. Instead I go to *Rush Hour 2*. Which is a pretty decent movie, actually."

"I take it Catherine wasn't really sick?" Amy asked.

"It turns out she was. She had mono and was out the rest of the semester," Ephram answered.

"So then you weren't geeky at all!" Amy exclaimed, a grin breaking across her face. "Gwen Stefani *was* gonna go out with you."

Ephram grinned back.

Then suddenly the smile slid off Amy's face. Her brown eyes widened. "Oh my God!" she cried, looking at the clock on the diner wall. "Is that the right time? We totally missed the bus!"

"It's okay. We'll catch the next one," Ephram said.

"No, we won't!" Amy shot back. "There is no next one."

"Oh. Well, that could be a problem," he admitted. *My dad is going to freak. And her dad is going to blame me for the whole thing,* Ephram thought. But he couldn't quite convince himself to feel bad about having to spend a bunch more hours alone with Amy. In fact he didn't feel bad at all.

CHAPTER 5

Another night, another dinner at Mama Joy's. At least it got Ephram out of the house. He'd been grounded after he and Amy cut school to go to Denver. Dr. Abbott and Dr. Brown had to drive all the way up there to pick them up and were none too pleased about it.

Ephram followed his father and sister up the driveway. Delia was about to drop the doggie bag that contained the piece of chocolate cake she'd taken only one bite of. Ephram smiled as he noticed his sister's gait; she was slowing down, getting more and more sleepy with every step. He wondered if she'd make it all the way upstairs into her room.

As usual the Great Dr. Brown walked right past the newspaper on the front lawn. Ephram was pretty certain that if he stopped picking up the *Everwood Pine Cone* every day, they would be two feet deep in useless paper before his father ever noticed. He scooped it up and gave it a cursory glance. Nothing much happened in Everwood, which meant that the town paper was basically full of . . . nothing.

"Log rolling finals are Saturday. Can't miss that," he informed his family. "But dear God, no! They're up against the library bake sale. How to choose?"

"They play logging highlights on cable access," his father replied, totally missing Ephram's sarcasm. "I'd go with the bake sale." He caught the doggie bag just as it fell from Delia's tired fingers and picked her up. "Time for bed."

Ephram rolled his eyes and followed them up the front steps to the open door.

The open door?

Instantly he was on guard. Why was it open? Who had opened it? His father stood still, staring suspiciously at the mangled screen door. Ephram stepped around it and peered at the hinges. They were broken. It looked as if the door had been kicked in. He glanced at his dad.

"You think someone's still in there?" he whispered.

His father responded by shoving the sleeping Delia into his arms. "I'll check it out."

Ephram swallowed hard, trying to calm his pounding heart. He felt a pang of fear as his dad disappeared into the darkness of the house. He'd

lived in New York City all his life and had never
been mugged or burgled. How could something like
this happen out here in the middle of nowhere?

The sound of breaking glass from the house
made him jump. Delia woke and squirmed in his
arms. Ephram lowered her to the ground. "Shh,"
he said, taking her hand. He had to go in and make
sure his father was okay. And he couldn't leave
Delia alone. "Hold on to me."

Slowly, he led her inside. One of the kitchen
chairs had been pushed over on to its side. Delia
squeezed his hand so hard it hurt.

"I have a large dog," his father's voice drifted in
from the family room.

Yeah, like that'll work, Ephram thought, fear
still coursing through him. A light went on in the
family room, and he heard his dad gasp. Delia took
off toward the sound. Ephram had no choice but
to follow. He skidded to a stop in the doorway.

In front of him stood his father, brandishing an
umbrella like a weapon. And in front of his father
stood a deer calmly chewing on the ficus plant next
to the couch.

"So much for vicious intruders," Ephram muttered, immediately feeling stupid for being afraid.

"Careful," his dad replied. "It might have a gun."

The deer was still there the next morning when
Ephram came down to the kitchen. He could see it
curled up peacefully on the porch, looking about

with its gigantic brown eyes. His father was yelling at it, waving his arms. The deer didn't even blink. Clearly this was not an animal that feared people.

"Maybe we should call animal control," he called out to his dad. "Might work better than yelling at her."

His father shrugged and headed back inside. "I think she'll wander back on her own," he said. "Till then she's welcome to our trash." He glanced at Ephram. "Which you're welcome to take out."

"Nice," Ephram muttered under his breath. His father had just been out on the porch, which was halfway outside. Why hadn't he brought the trash with him? Ephram stuffed the rest of his cookie in his mouth, grabbed the giant black trash bag, and slammed out the door. On the porch, the deer had gotten up and was chewing on his father's hammock. Ephram smiled to himself. He had a feeling his dad would be calling animal control after all.

But as he started down the steps with the trash, the deer suddenly lifted her head and looked at him, right into his eyes. Ephram stopped, surprised. This little wild animal stood not five feet away and gazed at him trustingly. He took in her twitching nose, her soft brown fur, her hopeful eyes. She was beautiful.

"Hello," he murmured. She cocked her head slightly and kept staring at him. Ephram felt a pang of sympathy. The poor thing was still just a baby, he could see. And she was so far from home, well, from wherever a deer was supposed to be. He could imagine how confused she must feel. "Little lost?" he asked her. "Tell me about it."

Mrs. Lippman couldn't be more of a stereotype if she tried. Short hair, sun-weathered skin, not an ounce of body fat, whistle hanging around her neck on a braided nylon cord, office decorated with trophies and team banners, and a metal supply closet stuffed with basketballs and volleyballs.

And Ephram's school folder open on her desk.

"You want to guess what we're doing here?" the gym teacher asked him.

Truthfully, he didn't have the slightest idea. "Um . . . you want to talk about sports?" he ventured. "I suck at team sports."

Mrs. Lippman gave him the tiniest of smiles. "You're seeing me in my guidance counselor capacity today," she said. "Small school, we tend to double up."

That explains the file, Ephram thought with a sinking feeling in the pit of his stomach. He'd been here only a month and already the guidance counselor was after him? He'd never even met the guidance counselor at his old school.

"Those my grades?" he asked, nodding at the offending folder.

"They are."

Ephram ran his fingers through his hair. He wasn't sure exactly how his grades were these days, but he was guessing that most of them hovered somewhere between failing and soon-to-be failing. "So I'm about to get a lecture."

This time Mrs. Lippman gave a real smile. "How about we call it information gathering. I'm trying to understand what's going on with you." She opened the folder and pulled out a small stack of papers bearing the letterhead of Ephram's school in New York. His old transcripts. "At your old school, your alphabet used to go from A to B, Ephram. But since you moved to Everwood, you've discovered all these nice new letters."

Ephram didn't bother to think about it much. Grades were pretty much at the bottom of his priority list these days, somewhere after remembering to wash his underwear every so often. "I'm having some trouble keeping up," he mumbled.

"Maybe that's because you haven't even taken your poetry text out of the shrink wrap yet," Mrs. Lippman said.

Ephram winced. He should've known Mr. Kamlet would rat him out.

"Two of your other teachers assumed you had a learning disability," the guidance counselor went on. "That's more than just not keeping up. That's not trying. So I guess this is a lecture—one I'd usually follow up with a call to your father." She waited until he looked up at her. "Do you think that would be a good idea?" she asked softly.

"Not if you're looking to improve the situation," Ephram answered. For a gym teacher, she was being pretty cool. He figured he might as well be honest with her.

Mrs. Lippman sighed. "Look, Ephram, you've had a tough year. Normally I'd applaud someone like you just for getting out of bed in the morning."

Which is not as easy as it sounds, Ephram thought.

"But I'm trained to look for trends, and right now you're trending downward," she finished.

Ephram knew she wanted an answer, but he didn't know what to say. He decided to go for sarcasm. "Trending downward? Is that like a technical term?"

She didn't back down. "It will be when they ask me why you flunked out," she replied.

He had no response to that. Were his grades really that bad? Did people actually flunk out of high school? A vague feeling of uneasiness washed over him. Only losers failed classes, right? Was he becoming a loser? He couldn't do anything but stare at Mrs. Lippman.

"That's all for now," she said. "You can go."

Wordlessly, Ephram stood and left the office. The usual frenzied end-of-the-day crowd of cliques and couples rushed by in the hallway, but for once he didn't care that he was alone. He made his way to his locker and absently spun the lock. His mother would be horrified if she knew about the conversation he'd just had. She'd never put pressure on him to do well in school; it had simply been understood.

He yanked the locker door open, almost slamming it into Amy, who appeared out of nowhere. He couldn't have been so out of it that he didn't notice Amy, could he?

"I need to consult you," she said, catching the door.

"I'm not sure I'm qualified to advise anyone right now," he muttered.

"But this is your specialty," she argued. "I need some fresh reading material. Thought I'd give one of your comics a whirl."

A little tingle of excitement made its way down Ephram's scalp. Girls just didn't ask about comics for no reason. Girls only pretended to like comics if they were interested in you, right? He looked up into Amy's gorgeous eyes. "I thought girls liked beauty magazines," he said, testing her.

She shrugged. "It's for Colin."

The tingle vanished instantly. Of course it was for Colin. Everything Amy did was for Colin. He jerked his gaze away from her and leaned into his locker so she couldn't see his face.

"I finished reading him *Call of the Wild* and I

need something easy on the eyes," she continued, oblivious to Ephram's pain. "Come on, lend me one."

Ephram forced himself to take a deep breath. It was stupid to think Amy was into him, but it wasn't every day he got to talk about comics, at least not since he'd left home. He pasted a smile on his face and turned back to Amy. "Sure," he said, unzipping his backpack. "We have an assortment of manga imports, although Japanese nonlinear storytelling might be a bit much for him."

Amy responded with one of her adorable little lopsided smiles.

"There's the latest Green Lantern," he offered. "Traditional good-triumphs-over-evil stuff."

Amy barely even glanced at the comic as she took it. "So . . . what did Mrs. Lippman want?" she asked casually.

Ephram's mouth dropped open. She'd seen him in the guidance counselor's office? So this whole comics thing had just been a ruse?

"Apparently my serve is off," he said curtly.

Her brown eyes were worried. "She noticed you broke the record, right?"

Ephram glanced around the emptying hallway. It was bad enough that he'd had to talk to Mrs. Lippman about his failures. He definitely didn't want to discuss his new loser status with Amy. So he went for the best answer he could think of. "Huh?"

"The record," Amy repeated. "For longest period of new-kid denial in the annals of County High."

"I knew this town had an underbelly, but I didn't know it had annals," he said, going for a light-hearted tone and completely failing.

"New kids get here, they usually spend the first few weeks treading water. You know, no new friends, coasting through classes, locker strangely undecorated. Like they're just here temporarily until their parents' divorce is final or whatever. Until they can go back to their *real* home."

Ephram busied himself with zipping up his backpack. He didn't want to admit how close she was to the truth.

"It works for like a month," Amy said gently. "But eventually they settle in."

He didn't look at her. "I won't be settling in," he said. "Not without a fight."

Ephram downed another cookie and watched as the animal control truck pulled into the driveway. It looked unthreatening enough, just a plain white truck. And his dad had told him the animal control people had promised that the deer wouldn't be hurt. But still he felt goosebumps prickle his skin. He shot a glance at the doe, who stood nibbling grass on the front lawn.

The animal control guy climbed from the cab of the truck and adjusted his belt over his sizable beer gut. He held up a hand in greeting as Ephram walked down the back steps to meet him.

"Got yourselves a deer, huh?" the guy said conversationally. He opened up the back of his truck and pulled down a ramp.

"Yep," Ephram replied. What else was he supposed to say? He watched as the guy looped a rope around the doe's neck and gently tugged it to get her moving.

"I don't see too many of these all the way from Mount McConnell," he told Ephram. "This is exciting."

"Uh, yeah, let me catch my breath," Ephram joked. "How do you know that's where she's from?"

The guy pointed at the deer's tail. "See that mark right there? Makes her a blacktail. Only a handful of those this side of Colorado, all from a wildlife preserve past the summit. She wandered a ways, all right."

Ephram nodded, watching as the guy coaxed the doe onto the ramp. "Long drive back?" he asked.

The guy nodded. "Few hours, then a lungbuster of a hike. Two days maybe."

"I hope you brought lunch," Ephram replied.

"Oh, I'm not taking her to McConnell," the guy said, laughing. "She's getting a lift as far as White River. I'll be back for happy hour at Taggerty's." He pulled on the rope, but the doe didn't budge. It was as if she'd put one hoof onto the ramp and realized that nothing good was going to come from her getting into this truck.

Ephram reached out and laid a hand on her soft back. "White River," he said. "Is that nice?"

The guy shrugged. "Sure. Not much escape cover, but it's real pretty."

Escape cover? Ephram wasn't entirely sure what that meant, and he wasn't entirely sure he wanted to know. But the doe looked at him with her big trusting eyes, and he had to ask. "Is that a bad thing?"

"It is when it's hunting season." The guy made a little clucking sound, trying to coax the deer up the ramp. She didn't move.

"Wait," Ephram said, panic building inside him. "Are you saying she might end up on someone's *barbecue?*"

The guy gave a good-natured nod. "I go out there this time every year with my brother. We bag enough meat in a half-hour to last all winter." He pulled harder on the rope. The deer took a tiny step forward, then another. Soon she would be in the truck and out of Ephram's life. He didn't have to worry about her. She wasn't his responsibility.

"Come on, Bambi," the guy said, leading her the rest of the way up the ramp.

Ephram sighed. He couldn't do it. He couldn't let this innocent little doe become someone's dinner just because she'd left home and gotten lost.

"Hold up a sec," he said. "Bring her back out."

The animal control guy frowned. "Say what?"

"I'll take her," Ephram said. "I'll bring her back home myself."

The guy stared at him as if he'd sprouted a black tail of his own.

"Can I keep the rope?" Ephram asked.

The second he heard the front door slam, Ephram knew what was coming. His father stomped into the kitchen and dumped two bags of Chinese food onto the table. "What is that?" he demanded, nodding toward the lawn where the deer was tied.

"A doe," Ephram said, trying to sound light-hearted. "A deer. A female deer—"

"All I asked you to do was to be home when animal control got here," Andy interrupted. Clearly he was in no mood for joking.

"I was here," Ephram said shortly.

His father frowned. "Did they come?"

"Oh yeah," Ephram said. He had no interest in making this easy. He turned on the water and began washing a carrot in the sink.

"Then why is she out there chewing on my mailbox?" Andy cried.

"Because animal control was gonna dump her on a rifle range," Ephram snapped. "Practically painted a bull's-eye on her ass."

He wasn't expecting his father to understand,

and he was right. The Great Dr. Brown threw his hands up in the air. "Well, what are we going to do with the damn thing? It can't stay here."

Ephram squared his shoulders. "I'm gonna take her home." He didn't have to look at his dad to know how that one was going to go over. He let the silence stretch out while he washed another carrot.

Finally his father spoke. "You do realize that deer live in the woods?" Ephram didn't bother to answer. "In the mountains?" his dad continued. "*Outside?* Where you don't go?"

"She's from a protected preserve a few hours from here," Ephram told him. "I already mapped it out. I'm gonna get a ride in the morning and then I'll have to hike up with her overnight."

He hadn't even finished his sentence when his dad began laughing. "You don't know the first thing about hiking," he said. "Forget about it. You're not going."

Typical. When would Andy realize that he didn't get a say in Ephram's decisions? "I am so," Ephram announced. He took the carrots and went out to feed Bambi.

She looked up from the mailbox as soon as she heard him coming, and moved right to him. When he held out a carrot, she gazed up at him for a moment before taking it gently from his palm. Ephram felt his heart squeeze a little. He had a better relationship with this wild animal than he did with his own father.

Right on cue, his dad came out of the house to join him on the lawn. Ephram didn't care. He was taking Bambi home, and no one was going to stop him.

"You can't shepherd a deer back to the mountains," his father said. "Don't be ridiculous."

"She has a home out there, she just needs help getting to it," Ephram said. "And I'm going to help her. How is that any more ridiculous than what you did?"

His dad's eyebrows shot up in surprise. "What did I do?"

He doesn't even realize the depth of his own insanity, Ephram thought. "You moved us to Everwood because of some psychotic sense of destiny. Well, now it's my turn. I'm supposed to do this. I don't know why. I just am." He met his father's eyes. "And I'm going to do it whether you like it or not."

There was a brief silence. Then his dad sighed. "Fine. I'm coming with you."

It took Ephram a few seconds to process that. His father wanted to come with him on the hike? To help do the thing he'd made fun of Ephram for wanting to do? "No way," he said.

"If you're camping, I'm camping," his dad said.

"I can handle this on my own," Ephram insisted.

"I am not about to let my fifteen-year-old, who doesn't know a pine tree from a baked potato, go exploring the tundra alone. So if you want to go, you better pack enough trail mix for two." He turned and went back inside, leaving Ephram alone with the deer.

Two days in the wilderness with his father. It was going to be a nightmare.

Ephram gazed at the rugged landscape as Irv drove the school bus around a particularly harrowing curve in the mountain road. He hated these curves. It was too easy to imagine the bus just tipping over sideways and plunging them all over a cliff. To distract himself, Ephram glanced at Bambi, standing placidly in the aisle between the seats. She still wore her rope leash. Ephram was wearing all-new GORE-TEX hiking clothes adorned with orange stripes. To his horror, his father was decked out in a matching outfit with new boots. Ephram had refrained from pointing out that the new boots were going to cause blisters within an hour of starting their hike. The man was a doctor; shouldn't he know things like that?

Irv pulled the bus over to the side of the road. In the distance Ephram could see the beginning of a trail. He turned to Irv and repeated back the directions the old man had given him. "Four miles west, eight more through Mountain Lion Pass—which I

really wish was called Mountain *Bunnies* Pass—
until we see the signpost at the pinyon-juniper
woodland, which we can't miss."

"And even if you do, you'll smell it," Irv said with
a smile. "Like nothing you ever smelled before.
Smells clean."

Ephram nodded his thanks and led Bambi off
the bus while his dad thanked Irv one more time
for baby-sitting Delia while they were gone. Why
couldn't he have just stayed with Delia himself? It
was beautiful up here; hiking in these mountains
would have been amazing if he didn't have to deal
with his father every step of the way.

He'd decided to deal with it by ignoring the
Great Dr. Brown as much as possible. He didn't
even bother waiting for him to get started. He led
Bambi straight toward the trailhead, figuring his
dad would catch up. Still, he couldn't help glancing
over his shoulder just to make sure. Irv tossed his
father a flare gun, and Ephram felt a stab of nervousness. Would they need that? The closest he'd
ever come to hiking was walking from one end of
Central Park to the other.

He glanced around at the trail, which plunged
almost immediately into a thick forest of trees so
tall they blocked out the sky. Would they get lost
out here?

"No," Ephram muttered to himself. He had
maps, and he'd memorized them. He knew Irv's

directions by heart. He would get the doe home with no problems.

"Okay, let's get going," his father said, walking briskly up behind him. Without hesitating, he stepped in front of Ephram and charged ahead, assuming he should lead the way, as usual. Ephram rolled his eyes. "Come on, Bambi," he said.

It took about an hour for Ephram to get completely and totally sick of his dad. First of all, he kept whistling. Second, he kept nagging Ephram to drink more water even though he'd already finished a whole bottle. And worst of all, he seemed oblivious to Ephram's bad mood.

"Zip your coat," Andy said, taking a break from the whistling at long last.

"I'm not cold," Ephram muttered. He turned to check on Bambi, who followed him like a giant dog.

"You will be in an hour."

Does he think I'm five years old? Ephram wondered. But he zipped his jacket. Sometimes it was just easier to give in than to fight. "For the record," he said, "you don't know anything about hiking either."

"I know you can't drink stream water."

Ephram rolled his eyes. "Everyone knows that."

"Know why?" his father asked. "*Giardia lamblia,* a protozoan-cum-waterborne-cyst with a nasty knack for twisting up mammalian duodena."

Great, Ephram thought. *Even in the wilderness, I can't escape his giant ego and his need to show off constantly.*

"I also know young Bambi here has four stomachs," his father rambled on. He named the stomachs and was going on to discuss how fast deer could run when Ephram finally couldn't take it anymore. "You're a neurologist," he interrupted. "Why do you know all this?"

His father glanced at him in surprise. "I read it in college."

"And what, you remember everything you ever read?" Ephram said, disgusted.

"Don't you?" his dad asked, brow knit in confusion. He turned and headed down the trail, whistling again.

Ephram stopped walking and stared after him. The guy was a brilliant surgeon *and* he had a photographic memory? That just wasn't fair. How was anyone supposed to live up to that?

"Fork in the road!" his father called cheerfully. Ephram shook off his annoyance and led the doe up to the split in the path. "I'm pretty sure the trail follows the creek, but check the map," he said.

He stroked Bambi's nose as his dad consulted the trail map. "Nope, it goes left," he announced.

Ephram looked up at the two trails. He had studied the map before they left, and studied it even more most of the way up in the bus. He felt certain they should go right. He *knew* it. "You sure?" he asked skeptically, reaching for the map.

"I used to navigate people's frontal lobes for a living," his father said, decisively folding the map. "I'm pretty good with directions." He took the leash from Ephram's hand and pulled Bambi after him down the lefthand trail.

Ephram swallowed down his fury. "Fine," he said through gritted teeth. "Left it is."

When they started going downhill, Ephram thought it was odd. But what did he know? He'd never navigated anyone's frontal lobe. Still, when they were still going downhill after an hour, he finally had to say something. "We've been heading down for a while, shouldn't we be going more . . . up?"

"It's a gradual ascent," his father answered confidently. He checked the handheld GPS gizmo he was so proud of. "We're right on track."

Bambi nuzzled Ephram's arm. He took her leash back from his dad. "She's looking at me funny, like she's thinking this doesn't look familiar."

His father chuckled. "She's a wild animal, she's thinking, 'Hi, are you made of food?' Keep up. We're making good time." The path was wide here, so he waited for Ephram to catch up to him. They walked side by side. Ephram was miserable.

"So, you making any progress with the Abbott girl?" his dad asked.

Amy. Just the thought of her made Ephram's

heart race. Why couldn't he be out here with her instead of his insufferable father? He didn't answer.

"I'm just asking," his dad said. "Are you still friends? Because you can cover a lot of groundwork from the friend zone."

"Lucky me, you remember a book on relationships you read in high school," Ephram snapped.

"Fine, something more my business then," Andy replied. "How's your schoolwork going?"

Mrs. Lippman's face flashed into Ephram's mind. Had she called home after all? Did his father know he was failing? He decided to go on the offensive— the surest way to distract his dad from this subject. "I guess I should be glad that you made it six hours before you tried to turn this into some kind of bondfest."

Bingo! His father's face fell. "I'm only trying to talk to you."

Nice, Ephram thought. *Schoolwork is forgotten*. "Well, don't," he said, walking faster.

Andy sped up too. "I breathe and it offends you. What did I do now?"

Ephram heaved a sigh. Why couldn't the man just be quiet and leave him alone? "Nothing," he said. "You've been great. Zip your coat."

"You're mad at me because I'm looking out for you?"

"First you try to parent me, then you want to be my buddy. And you're not good at either one,"

Ephram burst out. "It's bad enough you invited yourself along for the ride. Don't embarrass either of us by trying to leverage it."

"Would you rather go back to the way it was in New York?" Andy demanded. "When we never even spoke?"

Ephram laughed harshly. "It worked pretty good. I had a life, I could make my own decisions, do things I wanted from time to time—"

"Things you wanted?" his dad yelled. "I planned this trip for *you*."

"Who asked you to?" Ephram yelled right back. "I wanted to come out here and help the deer. You invited yourself along. You had to take over. Because you know everything and I know nothing. It's the story of our lives. Only these days it's worse because you're trying to make up for lost time."

He'd had it with his father. He couldn't even stand to walk next to him anymore. Ephram pushed aside a large branch and stormed ahead . . . out into the field where Irv had dropped them off this morning.

Just breathe, Ephram told himself. *Take a deep breath and calm down. You're not allowed to punch your own father*. Because that's what he wanted to do right now.

His dad stood next to him, staring at the trailhead in astonishment. "This looks vaguely familiar," he joked.

"We're right back where he dropped us!" Ephram shouted.

"At least we're not lost," his dad replied lamely. "The GPS must be busted."

Ephram just looked at him. The string of jokes and excuses was making him angrier by the second.

"I'm sorry, Ephram," his father added.

That wasn't good enough. Ephram spun away from him and squirmed out of the heavy backpack he'd lugged around all day. He threw it on the ground and began unpacking his tent while the deer tried to chew on the strap of the pack.

"Why are you unpacking?" his father asked.

"I'm setting up camp," Ephram told him. "Sun's coming down and we might as well start again fresh in the morning."

"We can still make good time if we—"

Ephram shot Andy a look filled with all the fury he could muster, and his father shut up. *Guess we know who's calling the shots around here now,* Ephram thought. But it didn't make him feel any better.

It was at least two hours before they spoke again. Ephram could feel his father watching every move he made—watching as he put up the tent wrong three times, watching as he gathered firewood, watching as he used up almost all of the matches without managing to start a fire. He could feel his father's need to jump in and tell him what he was doing wrong. But somehow, through some miracle, his dad managed to keep his opinions to himself, at least until Ephram's ninth try at starting the fire. He lit yet another match and placed it in the dry kindling. It sputtered and went out.

"You built it well," his father said. "But if you'd get the kindling under—"

"Don't," Ephram interrupted. "You are forbidden from dispensing advice on anything, ever. You're fired."

"There's some paper in—"

"Fired," Ephram repeated, raising his voice.

For one tense moment, his father looked as if he might argue. Then he held up his hands. "Fine," he said. "You drive."

Satisfied with his moral victory, Ephram struck another match. He guarded it with his hand as he lowered it slowly to the kindling and held it there as long as he could. The flame took, burning a tiny cluster of dry grass. Ephram felt a surge of pride.

Then the fire went out.

"Oh, come on!" he moaned. It was humiliating. Even his father's *silence* felt smug. Ephram stood up, grabbed his dad's pack, and pulled out the flare gun Irv had given them. He spun around, aimed it at the little pile of firewood and kindling, and pulled the trigger.

The flare shot out, practically exploding the pile. Ephram closed his eyes, fearing the worst. But when he dared to open them again, he saw the firewood burning merrily.

"That's one way to do it," his father said dryly.

Ephram couldn't help smiling. He tried to hide it by bending to put the gun away. There was no point in letting his father think they were buddies now. He pulled out the pack of sandwiches and divvied them up.

They ate in silence for a little while, until the doe ambled over and lay down near Ephram's backpack. She looked exhausted.

"She okay?" his dad asked.

"She will be. When she's safe."

"You can only do so much for her, Ephram. She may wander again."

Ephram sighed. He'd been trying to avoid that thought for two days. "I know."

His dad poked at the fire with a stick, creating a little blaze of warmth. "You were right, you know," he said. "About me trying to control everything. I do that."

Ephram nearly choked on his sandwich. "No. Really?" He let the sarcasm drip heavily, but his father just smiled.

"Your mom used to be the only one who could call me on it," Andy said.

Ephram could see that. Even though the Great Dr. Brown was . . . well, the Great Dr. Brown, it had always been Ephram's mom who ran the family.

Ephram had never even questioned it. He figured she was probably nicer to his dad about it than Ephram had been, though. The familiar pain constricted his throat. Plenty of people had told him that he was like his mother, but it surprised him to hear it from his father.

"It used to help me keep people alive, taking charge," his dad went on. "I always knew the right answer. It's an instinct I cultivated for surgery and it made me capable of doing things so . . . fantastic that I can't even take credit for them. I gave orders, things happened, and it was like I was watching from the mezzanine until later someone thanked me for saving them."

Ephram had heard him talk like this before, but it had always sounded egotistical. This time he got the feeling that his father really didn't mean to be patting himself on the back. There was a tone in his voice that Ephram had never heard before, as if his dad were trying to figure something out, something he'd never realized.

"It's hard to turn that off," Andy was saying. "The same compulsion everyone used to nurture in me . . . well, it makes me screw everything up now— for you, for Delia." He glanced up at Ephram and gave him a sad smile. "The last few months I feel like the only thing I've done right is help a few strangers get better and stop talking out loud to my dead wife."

Ephram felt a pang of guilt. The talking-to-Mom

thing had mostly embarrassed him. He'd never really thought about how it must feel for his father, trying to go on with life when his wife was gone. He looked into his dad's eyes. Maybe he could give the guy a break, just this once. "Well, that's something," he said.

The Great Dr. Brown's face lit up like he'd just opened the best Christmas present of all time.

"So you asked about school," Ephram went on.

"What about it?"

Ephram took a deep breath. "I'm not doing too well."

"*How* not well?" his father asked, a hint of his old know-it-all tone creeping back into his voice. Ephram shrugged, and his dad, who understood exactly what that meant, exploded. "That doesn't make sense!" he shouted. "You're an excellent student! You always have been—"

Ephram turned away. He should have known his father's vaguely human behavior was too good to last. But to his surprise, the rant instantly stopped.

"I'm doing it again, aren't I?" his dad asked. Ephram raised his eyebrows. "Okay. So why do you think you're having problems?"

"I'm not sure," Ephram admitted. "I'm having a hard time *trying*. I get up, I go. But I can't care. At first I thought I was just mad at you for moving us here. But now, it's like I left the part of me that cares about anything in New York. Anyway, my counselor says I'm trending downward."

He waited for the lecture. But instead of rant-
ing and raving, his father just looked thoughtful.
"People have funny ways of measuring progress,"
he said. "For what it's worth—and that might not
be very much—I'm impressed. And if you left any
part of you in New York, it definitely wasn't the
part of you that cares. Look where you are,
Ephram. Look at her."

Ephram followed his father's gaze to the doe,
who lay quietly nearby, trusting without knowing
why she was here or where he was taking her. He
cared about this little deer. He cared enough to
have dragged himself and his father out into the
middle of nowhere.

His father stood up and headed for the tent.
"Good night, son," he said.

When they reached the fork in the trail the next
day, Ephram took the lead and for once his father
let him. The terrain grew steeper and more rocky,
and they had to coax Bambi over a few rough
patches. By noon, Ephram felt as if his legs might
just collapse underneath him.

"Why aren't we there yet?" his dad asked.

"Because we're out of shape," Ephram replied.
He heaved in another lungful of the thin mountain
air. And it hit him: The air—it was like nothing
he'd ever smelled before.

"Do you smell that?" his father asked.

Ephram nodded excitedly. "It smells *clean*." He glanced around wildly and finally spotted it: the sign Irv had told them about, and the fence. "The preserve starts up here," he cried. "Come on." Still holding Bambi's leash, he began to run, his tired legs forgotten. They'd made it! He was finally going to bring her home! The doe sprinted alongside him as if she knew where they were, where they were going.

At the top of the hill, Ephram stopped, prepared to see the most beautiful nature preserve in the world.

Instead he saw black. Black dirt. Twisted black stumps of trees. The blackened skull of a giant buck. As far as he could see, the forest was burned. Utterly destroyed. Bambi's nose twitched as she danced nervously at the end of her leash.

"No wonder she left," his father said, coming up beside him.

Ephram felt tears building up behind his eyes. How could this have happened? He'd tried so hard to help the little deer and it was all for nothing! "She was supposed to be safe here," he cried. "She can't survive in this."

"Ephram, it's okay," his father said.

"No, it's not!" Ephram shouted. "Where's she supposed to go now? What's she gonna do?"

"We'll hike a mile up, find another patch of the preserve—"

"No!" Ephram interrupted. "That isn't her home!" He was starting to hyperventilate now. He couldn't stop himself. It wasn't fair. He'd tried so hard; weren't things supposed to work out if you tried this hard? "All I wanted to do was bring her home."

"You did, Ephram," his father said gently. "It's just gone."

The tears spilled out of Ephram's eyes and streamed down his cheeks. He didn't care. This sucked. It just . . . sucked. Homes weren't supposed to be gone. They weren't supposed to disappear and leave poor innocent babies without any place to feel safe and protected and loved. Ephram angrily swiped at his cheek, but it was useless. He couldn't stop crying. He knew it wasn't about Bambi, and he was pretty sure even his obtuse father had figured that out by now.

"She'll do what we did," his dad said. "She'll find a new home."

"Our home is in New York," Ephram sobbed. "With Mom."

"It was," his father agreed. "But she's gone now and we can't go back." He moved a step closer and put his arm around Ephram's shoulders. "We left New York because there's nothing there for us anymore. We had to leave. Because what you're holding on to is . . . this." He gestured out at the barren, devastated preserve.

It looked like Ephram's soul.

"I just want to go back," Ephram whispered.

His father pulled him into a hug and held on tight. "Me too."

It only took a few hours to walk around the burned patch of forest. When they finally stopped, the land was filled with pine trees instead of the juniper and pinyon of Bambi's home. There was a stream nearby, and they were still on the preserve. Ephram sighed. It wasn't perfect. It never would be. But it would be okay.

He turned to the doe and stroked her soft fur one last time. "Okay, Bambi," he murmured. "I know this isn't your old place, but it looks do-able to me. Then again, I used to go to school above Ninety-sixth Street. Anyway, there's no hunting up here, so you'll be safe. I'd love to tell you it's all gonna be all right. That's what everyone told me. But it's just not. You can stay here or go back, either way it's gonna suck. But figure at least when it sucks you know you're alive. So I guess what I'm saying is it's okay when everything sucks. It means you're *somewhere*."

The doe looked at him with the same sweet, blank expression she always wore. Ephram smiled. "Okay, last cookie." He pulled a cookie from his pack and fed it to her. Then he loosened the rope around her neck and pulled the leash over her head. "I gotta go," he told her. Bambi's nose twitched and she looked off into the pine forest.

Ephram turned and headed back to the trail, where his father was waiting.

"Everything okay?" his dad asked.

"As good as it's gonna be," Ephram replied sadly. When he looked over his shoulder for the deer, all he saw was her black tail disappearing into the woods. Maybe she would be okay after all. Maybe they both would.

As Irv's school bus rattled its way back to Everwood, Ephram couldn't help thinking of Amy. She was the only thing about this place that made him even remotely hopeful. If he was ever going to make a new home for himself, he had to start with Amy, and that meant telling her the truth.

He waited until his dad had collapsed onto the living room couch to nurse his blister-ridden feet. "Hey, Dad?" he said.

"Yeah."

"Just how out of the brain biz are you?"

His father shrugged. "I hadn't really thought about it. Why?"

Ephram didn't want to ask. He didn't want to even think about Colin, or about how much Amy wanted her boyfriend back. But as long as he kept quiet, he was lying to her. "Remember you asked how Amy's doing?" he said in a rush. "She's still pretty wrapped up in her boyfriend. The one in a coma. She asked me to ask you if you'd look at him."

He kept his eyes down, but he could feel his father staring at him. "When did she ask you this?"

Ephram sighed. No matter how he tried, he couldn't get anything past the Great Dr. Brown. "A while ago," he admitted.

"I see," his dad replied. "You'll probably have to tell her the truth about that."

Ephram knew what that meant. It was a bargain: His father would do what he asked as long as Ephram confessed the truth to Amy. It sucked. It could destroy the one good thing in his life. But it was the right thing to do. "Probably," he mumbled.

"Runs in the family, I guess," his father said. "Trying to control everything."

Ephram's head snapped up. He wanted to defend himself . . . but how? It was true. He'd been hoping that he could make Amy forget about the love of her life. He'd been hoping to control her feelings.

"Sorry about that," his dad added with a smile.

Ephram stared at the Abbotts' front door. He didn't want to knock. He wanted to turn around and slink away like the coward he was.

Pulling together all his courage, he knocked.

Dr. Abbott opened the door and looked him up and down with his trademark bemused sneer.

"You," he said. "Why do you look like you're about to vomit?"

"Because I might," Ephram replied.

"Amy!" Dr. Abbott yelled over his shoulder. He gave Ephram another once-over. "Remain outside, please."

Nice, Ephram thought. It was freezing outside. Luckily it didn't take long for Amy to get downstairs. She gave him a big grin, her hair still wet from the shower. She gave it a little tousle with the towel she carried, and Ephram thought for a second that he might faint from how beautiful she was.

"Well, well. The warrior back from his vision quest," she teased. "Did you find your spirit animal up there in the woods? Let me guess, you're a . . . marmot."

Why is she being so sweet and funny and gorgeous? Ephram thought. *She's making everything worse.* He forced himself to speak. "Listen. I have to talk for a minute and then you'll be pissed, but let me finish before you hate me, okay?"

Amy's eyes widened, but she nodded. "Go on."

Ephram stood frozen. He knew it was his turn to speak. He'd practiced telling her this all the way over here on his bike, and he knew it was the right thing to do.

So he decided to tell her about camping instead.

"We made SpaghettiOs, in the woods," he blurted

out. "Sandwiches too, but I took the SpaghettiOs can and put it right on the campfire—which I got started by the way—had to use a flare gun but still, I put the kindling together and—"

"Ephram," Amy interrupted. "Start again."

He sighed. "Right," he mumbled. "Okay. Thing is, I lied to you." He heard her sharp little intake of breath and it actually made his stomach hurt to know that he'd hurt her. "I fixed it," he rushed on, "but I lied. You asked me to see if my dad would look at Colin and I said I did but I didn't. My problem is—and this is really just one of a whole bus load—is I lost my home recently." Even thinking about his mother made his voice break. He cleared his throat. "I can't get it back. Took climbing a mountain to admit that. You were right. I came to Everwood and I'm just coasting. I haven't made anything for myself here, except you."

Amy made some kind of little noise in her throat, and he looked up at her hopefully. But her brown eyes were cold.

"You're what makes this home to me," he continued, praying for her to understand. "I was scared that if my dad helped Colin I'd lose that. But I get it now. Colin is *your* home."

Now her eyes were brimming with tears. Great. He'd destroyed her life. "So I asked my dad to look at him and he's gonna do it tomorrow. Not that that makes up for what I did, but it's happening." He took a deep breath. "I . . . I am so sorry."

Amy still looked ready to cry. She also looked ready to beat him to death right there on her doorstep. And deep, deep in her eyes he could see it: hope. Behind her sadness and anger, she looked wildly, uncontrollably excited to hear that Colin had a chance.

"Okay," she said. She turned back inside and shut the door behind her.

"Okay," Ephram replied.

CHAPTER 6

Ephram didn't know what to expect when he showed up at the auditorium the next day. He was supposed to help paint sets for the ballet recital. He'd gotten roped into it because he was playing piano at the recital too. It hadn't bothered him at the time, because it meant that he got to hang with Amy. But now, for all he knew, she was never going to speak to him again. He'd lied to her about the most important thing in her life.

The instant he stepped in the door, she called him over excitedly. Ephram tried to hide his smile, but his cheeks felt hot and he had a feeling he was grinning like a clown in spite of himself. He took a seat on the stage and Amy handed him a paint-brush and a diamond-shaped thing that looked as if it were made out of a wire hanger. "We're on leaf duty," she said, nodding toward a few open cans of paint. "You get your choice: yellow, red, or brown."

He peered into the can of brown. "I think I'd call it burnt sienna," he said, dipping in his brush. "Although I don't know that I'd call this a leaf."

Amy grinned. "Surprised to see you here. I thought they only paid you to play piano."

"You doubt my school spirit?" he challenged her.

She snorted. "Whatever. It's cool of you to help."

He was still smiling his stupid I'm-so-in-love smile. He couldn't stop. He couldn't believe she was being so nice to him after what he'd done. It was amazing. *She* was amazing.

"So . . . your first ballet solo, huh?" he asked.

"Yup." She waved her paintbrush around the auditorium, a streak of yellow paint snaking its way up her perfect wrist. "Every year it's a mad dash to get the best seats. You'd think it was a Paul McCartney concert; I've never seen middle-age people run so fast."

Sadly, Ephram could imagine the scene. "A high school ballet depicting the changing of the leaves— high point of the Everwood social season. Why am I not surprised?"

"The Flower Mart actually sold out last year," Amy said. "All the soloists get bouquets. Roses mostly."

Was that a hint? Did she want him to buy her roses? "Good to know," he said, trying to sound casual.

"Except me, I mean," she said quickly. "Well, I've never had a solo before. But Colin used to bring me flowers. Not my parents or anybody, just Colin."

And we're back to Colin, Ephram thought. *As usual.*

Amy checked her watch. Ephram raised his eyebrows, questioning, "Colin's parents' appointment's almost over," she explained, sounding nervous. Ephram suddenly understood. Amy had done all she could by asking him for his father's help. Now it was up to Colin's parents to decide what would happen next. Ephram knew he should say something comforting. As much as he didn't want to talk about Colin, he realized that Amy needed to.

"My dad's appointments usually last just long enough for whoever he's talking at to sign on the dotted line," he told her. "I swear I can't remember a single time someone said no when the Great Dr. Brown offered his help. Colin's surgery is a done deal."

She didn't look convinced. "I watched this show about comas on the science channel," Amy said. "It showed people who came out after a long time, like six months. Most of them hardly looked human. I remember this one man, his face was frozen in this silent scream, like that painting . . . and most of them had their hands all curled up, like Jennifer Hockaday in special ed."

Ephram didn't know what to say. He'd seen some of his father's patients come out in worse shape than that. Amy was obviously strong—strong enough to stay loyal to someone who'd been gone for months now. But would she really be able to handle it if Colin ended up like one of those people on the show?

"Don't take this the wrong way," Ephram said. "But are you sure you want him back if . . . I just mean—"

"I want him back," Amy insisted. "No matter what."

Ephram nodded and turned back to his brown leaf. Amy's mind was made up. Her first priority would always be Colin. No matter what.

When he got home that evening, his father was on the phone and dinner was nowhere in sight. He threw his backpack onto the kitchen table and yanked open the fridge.

"I understand," his dad was saying. Ephram strained to hear him. Was he talking to Colin's parents? "There's really no need to explain. . . . All right. We'll talk again then."

Ephram shut the refrigerator door. "Who was that?" he asked.

"Just . . . work stuff," his dad said distractedly. He came over and pulled open the fridge, staring into it much as Ephram had.

"Was it about Colin Hart?" Ephram pressed.

"It was, as a matter of fact." He pulled out a Tupperware container and began trying to pry off the top.

"What did they say?" Ephram asked, not really wanting to hear the answer.

"Oh . . . they've decided not to pursue the surgical option," his dad replied, opening the Tupperware and sniffing the contents.

"What?" Ephram cried.

His father made a face and crossed to the trash can to dump the leftovers. "You can hardly blame them. It's a tough decision."

Ephram couldn't believe it. It had never even occurred to him that Colin's parents would say no. He'd pretty much figured that once he asked for his dad's help, the Great Dr. Brown would step in and bring Colin back within a week.

"So that's just it?" he asked.

"Nothing's just it," his father said. "Colin's medical status is constantly evolving. Who knows, tomorrow, next week, next month could be a whole new ball game."

Who is this and what has he done with my father? Ephram wondered. Where was the ego? Where was the know-it-all attitude? Where was the outrage at people daring to turn down the help of the best neurosurgeon in the world? "You're just going to let it lie?" he asked, not even trying to keep the skepticism out of his voice.

"There's no point forcing the issue."

"This is a new thing, right? This whole laissez-faire country-doctor bit?" Ephram asked, getting more agitated.

"Doctors don't have all the answers, Ephram," his father said.

Ephram fought the urge to laugh in his dad's face. "You did," he pointed out.

"Sometimes parents have answers too," his dad said mildly. "Set the table, will ya?"

Ephram moved mechanically to the cabinet to get the plates. All these weeks of angst about Colin and Amy and his father . . . and this was how it ended? No miracle surgery, no Colin waking up, no Amy forgetting him in her rush of love for her restored boyfriend.

Amy. The thought of her reaction to this news hit him like a punch in the gut. She was going to be devastated.

The tile of the school hallway was cold and hard, but Ephram didn't mind. His hand flew over the page as he sat on the floor jotting down the song he'd begun composing the night before. Obviously he would have to play it for Amy, but he wanted her to have a written copy of it, too. As a memento. Of her first ballet solo . . . and of him. Colin wouldn't be here to give her roses, but at least Ephram would be here to give her his song. That had to count, right? Eventually she would get over Colin, and it wasn't impossible that she would turn to him. . . .

"Hey, Amy," someone called from down the hall. He looked up to see her five feet away, staring at the ground as she walked. Shoving the music note- book into his backpack, he jumped to his feet and went over to her. She barely acknowledged him.

"My dad told me last night," he said quietly. "I'm sorry, Amy."

When she spoke, her voice was flat. Shattered. "I shouldn't have gotten my hopes up." She kept walk- ing, looking down, alone in her grief. The sheer force of her misery silenced him for a moment. How could he help her?

He knew the answer. He hated it, but he knew it. He had to help her make sure Colin got that operation. "Once in a while back in New York a patient would say no to my dad. At first," he told her.

Amy glanced up at him for the first time. "Then what happened?"

"He'd persuade them he was right. Except . . . well, people are different here. They gotta know you twenty-five years before they trust you to change their tire."

Amy's face fell. "So you don't think he can con- vince the Harts?"

"I don't know. But maybe *you* can."

She searched his face. "Do you really believe that?"

Ephram could see the need in her eyes, the need for someone—anyone—to believe in her. And the way she felt about Colin, she just might be able to pull off a miracle or two of her own. "Yes," he said.

She nodded. Then smiled. A tiny smile, but it was definitely there. "Thanks, Ephram." She turned and hurried off down the hall, a renewed bounce in her step.

"'Thanks, Ephram, for getting my boyfriend out of a coma so I can forget about you entirely,'" he muttered. Being the nice guy sucked.

He'd decided to give Amy the written song before her ballet recital that night and tell her that he'd play it on command whenever she wanted. He was pretty much finished with the composition now, although he wanted to work on it a little before he committed the entire thing to paper. He got to dress rehearsal early so he'd have time to play it a few times on the piano in the auditorium.

Amy stormed up in the middle of the fourth bar. He'd never seen her so angry. "Why didn't you tell me?" she snapped.

Ephram's hands were still in place over the keys, ready to continue playing Amy's song. "What?" he asked stupidly.

131

"Your father turned them down."

It took a moment to process this. His father had turned who down? One more look at Amy's face gave him his answer. With Amy, it was always about Colin, so "them" must mean Colin's parents. But that still didn't make any sense. "What?" he said again.

"The Harts asked him to do the surgery on Colin but he said no."

Ephram shook his head. Clearly there was some gigantic misunderstanding at work here. "Why?" he demanded. "Why wouldn't my dad want to operate?"

Amy's eyes narrowed to slits. "You tell me."

He couldn't believe it. She thought he knew about this! She thought he'd lied to her—again. "That's impossible," he said with utter confidence. "My father's a jerk, but I've never heard of him turning anybody down before. He's never met odds he didn't like."

"Well, he didn't like Colin's," Amy interrupted.

"Are you sure you got this right?" Ephram asked, starting to get annoyed by her anger. "Because the guy I know would give his left nut to rescue a kid from a coma and be the town hero."

"The Harts told me," she said. She studied his face for a moment. "Are you sure he didn't say anything to you?"

"Like we've ever had a meaningful discussion."

"If you are lying to me, I will hate you forever," Amy said, her voice ice cold.

Ephram threw up his hands. "Why would I lie to you? You're the only person I care about in this whole stupid town!" He could see that she still wasn't sure whether to believe him. It was his own fault; he'd lied to her for weeks about his dad and Colin. "Amy, I swear," he said. "I didn't know. I guess now we can both hate my father."

Amy avoided him after dress rehearsal, and Ephram couldn't blame her. He could blame his father, though. Of all times for the famous ego to fail, why did it have to be now? Why did it have to be something that mattered to Amy? He fumed all the way through getting dressed in his uncomfortable suit for the recital, and he was still fuming as he tried to do his tie in front of the hall mirror. His father came over and reached for the clumsy knot.

Ephram jerked away. "I got it."

His dad mercifully backed off, but he still seemed clueless. "Is Amy nervous about the recital?" he asked, as if he hadn't just destroyed her entire life.

"She's too pissed off," Ephram said.

"These are difficult decisions," his dad said. "What the Harts decided—"

"The *Harts*?" Ephram interrupted. Outrageous. Was his father actually going to stand here and lie to his face? "What *you* decided for them. This is so typical. The one time it matters, you back out."

"It *always* matters," his dad growled. "It just so happens that this time it matters to *you*. That doesn't mean that I can—"

"Amy matters to me!" Ephram cried. "And pathetic as this may be, you were her only shot. See, she's not used to being let down by you yet."

His father winced at those words, which sent a tiny sliver of satisfaction through Ephram. To his surprise, his dad didn't back down. "Ephram. They asked me what I would do if it were my son. I told them I thought it was risky. It's always tempting to leap in and try to surgically 'fix' things, but that's not always—"

"That's a load and you know it," Ephram said. "If it were your son? If it was me? You'd let me sit there in a coma when there was a zillionth of a percent chance you could ride in on your white horse and save me? I don't think so. If I didn't know better, I'd think you were just scared."

The wince was even bigger that time. His father looked shell-shocked. "Ephram . . ."

"We're gonna be late," Ephram said. He stalked over to the door and he didn't look back.

They rode to the high school in silence. Even Delia was out of sorts. As soon as his father stopped the car, Ephram sprang out and headed into the building without a word. Once inside the bustle of last-minute preparations and backstage nervousness, Ephram began to calm down. This ballet performance reminded him of his own recitals in the past, everyone warming up, practicing, feeling jittery and excited and terrified all at once. He checked over his sheet music, making sure everything was in order. Then he checked the rolled-up piece of music in his pocket. It was Amy's song. He'd tied it with a red silk ribbon.

The buzz of voices in the audience had grown to a fever pitch and the recital was starting in ten minutes. Ephram knew if he was ever going to give Amy her song, he had to do it now. Swallowing his nervousness, he made his way through all the tittering ballerinas, heading for the soloists' "dressing room," one semi-secluded corner behind a few old sets.

As he walked, he passed Mrs. Hart, Colin's mother, coming the other way. She nodded hello at him, but she didn't smile. She looked kind of ill, in fact. *What was she doing backstage?* Ephram wondered. *Had she been with Amy?*

Walking faster, he headed straight over to where Amy sat in front of a dingy mirror. She looked just as ill as Colin's mom. She was staring at a large, gorgeous bouquet of flowers on the counter in front of the mirror, and she seemed dazed.

Ephram stopped, unsure what to do. Had Colin's mother brought those flowers? That was really nice. But it was also kind of . . . creepy. Like getting flowers from beyond the grave or something. Colin wasn't here to bring flowers himself. That's what no one in this town wanted to admit, apparently. *Colin wasn't here.*

"Amy?" he asked. She didn't answer. She just gazed at those flowers as if she were in a trance. "Amy, what is it?"

"He's not coming back," she whispered.

Ephram felt a rush of guilt. He'd just been thinking the same thing. But he was pretty sure that thought had never even occurred to Amy before. "You don't know that," he stammered. "He could come out of it. He . . . he probably will."

His words were empty and they both knew it. She looked directly into his eyes. "He's gone," she said. And then her eyes glazed over and she wasn't there anymore.

Ephram's heart began to race. Amy looked seriously strange. As if she'd gone into shock or something. She was still sitting up straight, still looking in his direction. But she wasn't there. Her face was a blank.

"Amy," he said, taking a step closer. She didn't respond, didn't even move a muscle. "Amy?"

No response. Just . . . nothing.

Without hesitating, his heart pounding with fear, Ephram turned and sprinted through the backstage area, out onto the stage, and right up to the closed curtains. He pushed them aside, fighting his way through the heavy material. Immediately, he spotted Amy's parents sitting in one of the front rows. His dad and Delia sat behind them.

Ephram jumped off the stage and made a beeline for Dr. Abbott. Of course, his own father leaned forward, assuming Ephram was looking for him. "Ephram," he said. "Did you find Amy—"

Ephram ignored him and spoke to Dr. Abbott. "You have to come back there."

Amy's father looked startled. "What's wrong?"

"It's Amy," Ephram said in a rush. "She's—"

But Dr. Abbott was already up and running. Mrs. Abbott scrambled out of her seat and followed him. Ephram glanced up at his father, who was getting up, too, and they took off after Amy's parents.

Backstage, Amy was sitting right where he'd left her, staring straight ahead at nothing. Ephram heard her mother's gasp. "Amy!" she cried. Amy didn't answer. Dr. Abbott knelt in front of her, peering into her eyes. "Amy?" he said calmly. "Can you hear me?"

Nothing.

Ephram felt his dad come up behind him, but for once Andy kept quiet. Dr. Abbott picked Amy up in his arms. "We're going home," he announced, turning toward the backstage door. Mrs. Abbott grabbed Amy's ballet bag, gave Ephram a panicky-but-grateful smile, and went after him.

Ephram turned to see his dad watching all this, his face pale and drawn. He looked surprised, and it made Ephram furious. How dare he be surprised? Hadn't Ephram told him how important Colin was to Amy? How important he was to this whole town?

This was all his father's fault. "Nice going," Ephram hissed. Then he went after the Abbotts to help them to their car.

His father didn't try to follow him.

After school the next day, Amy came bouncing up to Ephram's locker. Her cheeks were pink, her brown eyes sparkling. Ephram didn't know what to think.

"You look better," he said.

"I feel better."

"Really?" he asked.

"I'm totally fine," Amy chirped. He'd never seen her so *up* before. He didn't want to ruin her new good mood, but still he felt he had to say something about what had happened. This was all just too strange.

"Last night was pretty—"

"Freaky, right?" Amy interrupted. "It's funny because the exact same thing happened to me once before, when we went on a family trip and I didn't have time to study for Mr. Burney's chem test? I just spazzed out. I just lost it. I guess it's good I got it out of my system, right? I feel totally fine now. I'm so embarrassed that everyone saw me like that, it's *so* not typical of me."

Her eyes were roving the hallway as she spoke, and Ephram got the feeling that she didn't even know what she was saying. "You're talking faster than my brain processes language," he told her.

"Oh, sorry," she said with a little giggle. "I'm a little bit . . . anyway, so how are *you*?"

Ephram shook his head. "How are *you*?" He wasn't going to let her get away with pretending everything was normal when it so clearly was not. "How are you really?"

"I'm completely fine," she said. "Really. I am."

"If you're not, you can tell me," Ephram said.

"I just told you I am." She was beginning to sound annoyed. Ephram didn't let that stop him.

"And if you ever want to talk about . . . whatever, I'll be—"

"Oh my God," Amy cried. "I totally forgot. I told Kayla and Paige I'd meet them out front to go to the mall. I gotta go." She took off at a run.

"I'll be here," Ephram finished as he watched her go. It was true, even though Amy clearly had no interest in hearing it.

By the next day, though, she'd come down a little. He could tell by the way she walked when he saw her in the hall and by the way her face lost its happy expression whenever she thought no one was looking at her. She didn't come over and talk to him, though. He just kept an eye on her from a distance.

During study hall, he wandered into the auditorium. The ballet had gone on two nights before, minus Amy's solo, and now the sets were half-demolished. Ephram sighed. He'd tossed out the crushed roll of music he'd intended to give her. It was useless now. He felt as if everything he wanted to do for Amy was useless. Only his father could help her, and the Great Dr. Brown wouldn't.

He sat at the piano and began to play Amy's song to the empty auditorium. She'd never hear it now, but he still thought of it as her song. He closed his eyes and let the music take over.

"What are you playing?"

Ephram jumped, startled. Amy stood beside him. "Nothing," he said quickly, embarrassed that she'd found him in one of his musical trances.

"Did you compose this 'nothing'?" Amy asked.

"What are you doing here?" he countered, changing the subject. "There's no practice."

"I had a free period so I thought I'd—" Amy stopped abruptly. "No, that's not true. I came because there's something I wanted to tell you. Yesterday, when you asked me if I was okay? I wasn't. I'm not. I'm *not* okay."

Ephram was afraid to speak. He didn't want to scare her off. He had a feeling that she needed to tell someone what she was going through and that she just might explode if she didn't.

"I remember in fourth grade Miss Kitzlinger's class and Mrs. Barber's class took a field trip to the brewery. On the way back I got onto the wrong bus. Colin thought they had left me behind. He walked back three miles, by himself, and stayed at the brewery till nightfall, trying to find me. Scared his parents to death. He just couldn't leave me behind."

Ephram hated this. All he wanted was for Amy to move on, to let go of Colin. But what he wanted and what she needed were two different things. "You won't leave him behind, Amy," he promised her. And he believed it. If there was one thing he'd learned about Amy, it was that she was never going to leave Colin behind.

"What were you playing before?" she asked.

Ephram blushed. "Just . . . just a—"

"Don't lie to me," Amy said.

He couldn't blame her for saying that. He'd lied to her before. So he steeled himself, and told her the truth. "You said no one gave you flowers but Colin. But it was your first—would have been your first—solo. I wanted to make sure someone remembered. So . . . I, uh, wrote a song for you."

Amy was silent for a moment. He couldn't tell if she was touched or if she just thought he was the biggest dork in the world.

"Will you play it for me?" she asked.

"It's not finished," Ephram began.

"Please." Amy's voice was low and throaty, her eyes pleading. There was no way he could refuse her. He began to play.

He didn't expect it to happen with Amy standing right there, but somehow the music just drew him in. He let his eyes close, and he let the melody wash over him. He was one with the music, just like he used to be when his mother was alive. He didn't focus on his hands moving over the keyboard; instead he just concentrated on Amy, on her sadness, and her beauty, and the way she made him feel like himself again even in this strange, remote place.

After he finished, he kept his eyes closed for a moment, trying to readjust to the silence. He felt Amy's hair brush his arm, her lips brush his cheek. "Thank you," she whispered.

When he opened his eyes, she was gone.

Ephram made his way home after school, the music running through his head as he steered his bike along the winding roads. It was a complicated song, the way Amy was a complicated friend. No matter how frustrated he got, her situation was always worse than his. What if it were Amy in the coma? Would Ephram feel any differently about her? He knew the answer: No. Amy might be developing new feelings for Ephram, but that wouldn't change her old feelings for her childhood love. Maybe it would always be this way: him wanting Amy, Amy pining for Colin.

His father was waiting for him in the kitchen.

"What?" Ephram said, taking in his dad's excited expression.

"I talked to the Harts again," the Great Dr. Brown reported. "I'm going to perform surgery on Colin."

CHAPTER 7

The minute Ephram woke up on Friday, the Colin clock began in his head. *One more day until Colin's surgery.* It had been like that ever since his father agreed to do the surgery. Everyone assumed it would be a miracle. Nobody gave one serious thought to the possibility that his dad would fail. As had come to be expected, the Great Dr. Brown would perform history-making surgery, and soon Colin would be back.

Colin . . . and no Amy. That was the part Ephram didn't want to think about. He wanted the surgery to go well. He just didn't want to face what was going to happen afterward. The famous Colin Hart back at school, back with Amy. For everyone else in town, it would be as if things finally got back to normal. But for Ephram, it would be as if things suddenly became bizarrely abnormal.

At school, Amy was too nervous to eat. She was pretty much too nervous to do anything. She told Ephram that she'd be spending the day of the surgery at the hospital with Colin's parents. But other than that, she seemed only vaguely aware that Ephram existed. Ephram decided he better get used to it.

He couldn't be honest with Amy about how he was feeling anyway. He wasn't terrified, or worried, or even a little bit nervous. His father performing surgery—it was like an eagle soaring or a Porsche driving a hundred miles an hour. It was what the man was created for, what he was placed on earth to do. The surgery would go well. And as for Ephram, he was excited.

Dr. Brian Holderman was coming that night. He'd be assisting in Colin's surgery the next day. And that meant at least one night of having fun and feeling normal again, enjoying the company of an old friend who would find Everwood every bit as strange as they did.

Ephram tapped the silverware together impatiently as he set the table for dinner. Uncle Brian had managed to do the impossible: be friends with the Great Dr. Brown *and* his son. Ephram couldn't remember a time when a visit from Uncle Brian had been anything other than a blast. And right now, a visit from *anyone* in New York would be enough to make him happy.

Ephram's dad glanced at his watch. Brian was late. Very late.

"You let a guy who's never been out of New York drive a car in the wilderness," Ephram pointed out. Their visitor could be anywhere. One thing about New Yorkers: They never drove. They could tell you how to get anywhere in the city on the subway, but they couldn't drive their way out of a paper bag.

His father shrugged. "It's Uncle Brian, not Woody Allen."

"Still—," Ephram began, but Delia's squeal cut him off. She ran to the door and yanked it open just as Brian was about to knock. His handsome face lit up in a huge smile, and he dropped the shopping bags he was holding in order to scoop Delia up into a hug.

Then he turned to the others. "Gentlemen and lady, worship me," he announced. "For I have brought unto you . . . New York City!"

He gave Ephram's dad a handshake-hug, then grabbed the shopping bags and began pulling out gifts like some kind of hip New York Santa. "Let's see, I've got two bags of H and H bagels, some Ray's pizza—individually wrapped for travel, no need to thank me."

"Did you leave anything behind for the actual New Yorkers?" Ephram's dad joked.

"No," Brian said. "I've got some Zabar's Special

Blend, Yonah Schimmel knishes . . . and a Brooklyn Cyclones hat for Delia. They're a Mets—"

"Minor league team that plays on Coney Island," Delia finished for him. "Thanks, Uncle Brian!"

Ephram took in all the reminders of home. Just thinking about real New York pizza made his stomach rumble. "For the longest time I was *upset* about not being in New York. Now I can finally know true despair," he said.

Brian laughed. "Despair's right up your alley. You're a musician."

"Not really these days," Ephram admitted.

"When you hear what I brought you, you're going to want to rededicate yourself," Uncle Brian said, pulling out an old album. "Bill Evans, on vinyl. It'll change your life, man."

Ephram felt a rush of affection for his old friend. He finally opened his arms and gave Brian a hug. It had been so long since he saw anyone from home that he actually felt tears coming on.

Brian turned to Ephram's dad. "Boss, I can't believe it. What's it been, now, a year since you and I stood over an open skull?"

Instantly Ephram's good mood vanished. Colin. Even with Uncle Brian, it was all really about Colin.

"It's been long enough to have blotted out some of your more colorful expressions," his father was saying.

"And tomorrow, once again, we'll hear the sweet sound of that drill digging away—"

Ephram was used to Brian's way of describing surgery. He'd heard it all his life. But somehow the gory details seemed a bit more gory when it was Colin's skull being discussed. Luckily his dad seemed to feel the same way. "Let's save the shop talk for after dinner," he said.

"Great," Brian said. "Start shoveling whatever you got onto my plate. And Ephram? Come outside and help me."

Ephram followed him to the door. "More bags?" he asked.

Brian shushed him. "I can't get the car to turn off," he confided. Ephram grinned as he followed Brian out into the fresh mountain air. For one tiny second, he felt like his old self—the Ephram from New York, the Ephram who had a mother—and he had a glimpse of normalcy again.

When he went to bed that night, he noticed his dad sitting with Brian out on the back porch, smoking a cigar and finishing up the Ray's pizza. Ephram cracked open his window so he could hear them talking. He didn't know what made him eavesdrop; maybe just the odd expression he'd caught on his father's face a few times during the evening—a sort of pinched look when he looked at Delia and Ephram.

Their words drifted up to him through the cold

night air. They were talking about Colin. About the surgery. Ephram let the technical terms wash over him; he'd never bothered learning anything about his father's work. But then Brian's tone changed, taking on a seriousness Ephram had never heard from him before.

"I can't help wondering why I'm here," Brian said. "I'm flattered you wanted me, but the Hart kid's team was available. I checked around. They're tops. Good doctors."

"I thought it would be good to have a familiar, trusted face in the room," Ephram's dad replied. "I was hoping for someone better looking, but you were the only one available."

Brian's silence proved that he wasn't falling for Andy's jovial tone any more than Ephram was. It hadn't occurred to him that there was anything strange about Uncle Brian coming to assist in Colin's surgery, but obviously there was. After all, since when did the Great Dr. Brown admit he needed help? An uncomfortable heaviness settled in Ephram's stomach.

From below he heard his father heave a frustrated sigh. "You might say I have performance jitters."

"You've been dormant," Brian replied. "It's normal."

"Not for me." Ephram didn't hear a trace of ego in his father's voice. It was simply the truth. Jitters while performing delicate brain surgery? Something for normal mortals, not for him. "Anyway, I may need to rely on you tomorrow more than usual if we're gonna have a shot at—"

"*If?*" Brian interrupted. "A *shot*? Boss, you're talking like you've never done this before."

"I haven't. Not this exact surgery."

"Like there's any order of difficulty in the miracles you've performed?" Brian asked. Ephram hung on his every word. He'd never heard his father sound so tentative before. As much as he hated the guy's usual know-it-all attitude, this self-doubt was . . . well, it was terrifying. Everyone was counting on him— Amy and Bright, Colin's family, all of Everwood. Not to mention Ephram and Delia, every day of their lives.

"I'm a different person now," his father was saying. "I may just be out of miracles."

"No, you're not," Brian said with utter conviction. Ephram took a shaky breath. Uncle Brian knew what he was talking about. He had to. "Before you took me under your wing, Andy, I never believed there were people who were put on this earth simply to fix God's mistakes. That's the sort of gift that doesn't go away."

Ephram watched as Brian stood and patted his father on the back. "Sleep easy, Dr. Brown," he said. "You're gonna be great."

A chill ran through Ephram. He'd been so busy

thinking about Amy and her needs that he hadn't noticed how truly frightened his father was. *Maybe it's like me with the piano,* he thought. Maybe when he lost his wife, the Great Dr. Brown stopped being able to be the Great Dr. Brown. He lost the will to use his genius, or maybe he lost the self-confidence. Whatever was causing it, one thing was perfectly clear: Ephram's father needed help.

Ephram woke at four in the morning and snuck past the bathroom. His dad was already in there, getting ready for surgery with Delia's help. Ephram felt a pang as he watched them—Delia handing grooming supplies to his dad like a nurse handing over scalpels and drills on command.

"Hair brush," his father said.

"Hair brush," Delia replied, slapping the brush into his outstretched hand.

Ephram continued down the hallway and jogged down the stairs into the kitchen. Delia had always had that little ritual with their dad. Every time he'd had a surgery scheduled, she'd get up and help "prep" him. Ephram, on the other hand, had always ignored the entire thing, pretending he wasn't even aware of his father's famous feats in the operating room.

But he'd never really been oblivious. He'd known perfectly well what his father was doing, and when, and to which patient. And he'd known all the other little rituals involved, too. Like his mom getting up to make breakfast, even when the surgeries started so early that breakfast came in the middle of the night.

By the time his dad came downstairs, Ephram had the bagels toasted and the coffee made. "Butter or cream cheese?" he asked.

His father looked stunned to see him there. "Ephram, you didn't have to do this."

"I was up," Ephram lied.

He noticed his dad's tense shoulders relax ever-so-slightly. "Cream cheese would be great."

Brian came in with Delia and a stack of tapes, which he set down in front of Ephram's father. "Oh, man," his dad said, breaking into a grin. "You brought them?"

"You know," Ephram offered, "there was this invention a few years back called the CD. Heard of it?"

His dad was shuffling through the stack of tapes. "These are the mix tapes your mom made for our surgeries. She'd figure out what songs to pick based on the kind of surgery we were doing. For instance, 'Glioma '97' had an upbeat, Motown kind of feel. Whereas 'Triple Aneurysm '99' is more of an angry lesbian with a guitar mix. And there's my personal fave, 'Middle Fossa Skullbase Tumor 2000.'"

"So which one do you want for today?" Brian asked.

"Bring 'em all. We'll figure out what we want on the drive."

Ephram went over to the counter and picked up the CD he'd made last night. "Here, add this to your collection," he said, tossing it to his father. "I call it 'Brain Stem 2002.'"

"You made this?" His dad's mouth was hanging open in astonishment.

"I was fiddling around with my iTunes," Ephram said. He didn't want it to turn into a big hugging-type situation. "It's no big deal. I'm going back to bed." He turned and fled.

The phone rang at seven-thirty. Ephram was still in his pajamas, although Delia had gotten dressed and gone over to spend the day next door with Nina, who always watched her after school. Ephram grabbed the phone.

"Hello?" he grumbled. *And why are you calling this early?* he thought.

"Hey," said Amy.

Ephram's brain couldn't seem to send any words to his mouth. He was too shocked. Why was Amy calling *him* on the day of Colin's surgery?

"Ephram?" she said. "It's Amy."

"Hey!" he said. "Hi. How are you?" *Okay, calm down,* he told himself. *Act like a normal human.* "Um . . . are you at the hospital already?"

"Yeah, but nothing's happening yet," Amy replied.

"I guess they're prepping him or something. Whatever that means."

"Probably shaving his head," Ephram explained. Amy's shocked silence alerted him to the fact that he was a moron for saying something like that so casually. He'd grown up around people who treated brain surgery as if it were a commonplace occurrence. But Amy wasn't used to thinking of Colin in those terms. She probably hadn't even realized that they'd shave his head. And the image of them doing it probably brought up other images she hadn't considered, like of doctors sawing into Colin's skull. Like all the other realities of brain surgery that nobody ever wanted to think about.

"Or, you know . . . I don't know what I'm talking about," he said lamely.

"So what are you up to today?" Amy asked, clearly needing a subject change. "Anything fun?"

"Not really. Gotta finish some math homework, read a few comics, eat lunch." *Could I be more of a complete loser?* Ephram wondered. "I'm falling asleep just listening to myself," he added.

"Sounds kinda nice to me." Amy sounded so sad. He decided to dispense with the small talk.

"Are you doing okay?" he asked.

"I don't know," Amy replied. "But this is what I've been waiting for, so it's a good thing. Right?"

"Yeah. I guess." What was he supposed to say? How could anyone know whether this was a good thing or not? They wouldn't know until Colin woke up . . . or didn't. Even then, they wouldn't really know for sure.

"Anyway, I should go," Amy said.

"No, wait, Amy—," he began. He was horribly aware of the fact that he hadn't managed to cheer her up at all.

"It's okay. I should stay close to the OR in case there's news. I just wanted to touch base with 'normal' for a minute."

Ephram smiled. He was her touchstone? That didn't sound so bad. "You definitely called the wrong person for that," he joked.

"I'll talk to you later, Ephram."

"Amy . . . ," he said. But she'd already hung up.

Ephram put the phone down and let sadness wash over him. He felt sorry for Amy, all alone in some hospital in Denver. He knew Colin's parents were there, but that hardly seemed like good company. Her own parents weren't with her. Even Bright hadn't gone to the hospital. But still, Ephram felt more sorry for himself. Amy was having a stressful day, but she'd probably get a good outcome at the end of it. For him, the outcome would suck.

Ephram sighed. "What kind of crappy friend am I?" he murmured. He already knew the answer. He wanted to be Amy's friend. He wanted to be *more* than that, of course. But if it came down to being friends or being Amy-less, the choice was clear. Even when things were awkward between them, he had more fun being with Amy than he did any other time in Everwood. He knew what he had to do.

He ran upstairs and got ready to go to Denver.

Amy stood in front of a vending machine, her money inserted, staring blankly at the rows of candy bars. It took Ephram about two seconds to figure out that she'd just come to the machine to give herself something to do. She didn't want candy. She wanted a distraction.

"You're holding up the line," he said.

She jumped and turned with an apologetic expression. Her brown eyes widened. "Ephram! What are you doing here?"

"I wanted a Twix."

She glanced at the vending machine and grinned. "You came a long way."

"Well, they're two to a pack, and I really only wanted one," he told her. "So I needed somebody to share it with."

Amy shook her head, still smiling, and pressed the button for a Twix bar. She bent to fish it out of the bin, grabbed her change, and led the way toward one of the small round tables nearby. "So how's the math homework coming?" she asked.

"Awesome. I never realized how much fun binomial equations could be." Ephram took off his backpack and dropped it onto a table. He tugged on the zipper.

Amy watched him in horror. "Wait. We're not seriously going to do homework right now, are we?"

"We could," he said, enjoying her panic. "But no." He pulled out the games he'd brought to help pass the time. "We've got Travel Scrabble, Travel Boggle, Travel Checkers, or Clue."

"There's no travel-size Clue?" Amy asked.

"Professor Plum wouldn't look as cool all squashed up and tiny," he explained as if he knew what he was talking about. "Take your pick."

"Scrabble," she said, grabbing the game.

"Excellent choice." Ephram reached into his backpack again and got out a mini-dictionary. "In case I have to challenge you. Never say I don't come prepared."

Amy laughed. Ephram didn't know who was more surprised to hear the laughter, him or Amy herself. She sat down and began setting up the game. "You must have *lived* at the hospitals back in New York, huh?"

"Actually, this is the first time I've been at the hospital when he was working," Ephram replied, feeling a stab of guilt as he said it. His father was the best neurosurgeon in the country, and he'd never even bothered to support him even a little bit? He shook off the guilt and concentrated on Amy. "Okay. Pick your letters."

She began choosing tiles, then stopped. "You're a good friend, Ephram," she said.

He glanced up at her, finding it hard to breathe through the sudden constriction in his throat. The way she was looking at him—it was as if he'd done something heroic. If this was being just friends, he'd take it. "So are you," he told her.

And they began to play.

By the time darkness fell, they'd played every single game at least once. They'd wandered from room to room and ended up in the cafeteria. Ephram had completed an inventory of all the pets his family had ever thought of getting—even though they'd never actually had one. Amy was on her fifth cup of tea. Ephram was out of conversation ideas. And Colin was still in surgery.

Amy checked her watch.

"I'm really not this boring," he told her. "It's just rare that I talk to any one person for so long. Most of the time I get in, I get out, no one gets hurt."

She gave him a tired half-smile. "It's not you. It's just . . . this day is starting to feel longer than the four months Colin's been in a coma."

"God, four months," Ephram repeated. He couldn't imagine how Amy had been able to survive that much time still loving someone who wasn't really there, but wasn't really gone.

"I know," she said. "Seasons changed. School started."

"The good part is, you'll have things to say to him when he wakes up," Ephram told her, trying for a cheerful tone. "You can tell him all about the strange new kid who moved to town."

"Right."

Wow, Ephram thought. *Not even a laugh.* "Now it's official," he announced. "I'm out of things to say."

Amy just nodded.

He was too tired to keep pretending to be a cheer-leader-type. It didn't come naturally to him, and he'd been at it for hours. He decided to act like himself instead. "What are you thinking about?" he asked.

"About the moment when he finally does wake up. I've thought about it a billion times."

"Yeah?"

"And I know what I'm going to say. It's not what you think," she added. "I'm going to tell him how sorry I am."

She was right. That's not what he would've thought. "Sorry?"

Amy gazed into his eyes, as if she were trying to figure out how much to trust him. "There's a whole part of this thing I haven't told anybody about."

"What?" he asked, not exactly sure he wanted to know any more intimate details about the life of Amy and Colin, couple of the millennium.

"We had a fight that day," she said in a low voice. "Before he took the truck. A big fight. I told him that I loved him."

"You guys have a weird way of fighting."

"He didn't say it back."

And there it was. What Ephram had been waiting for ever since the first day he met her: proof that her perfect romance wasn't perfect. Proof that Colin was not the guy for her. Proof that she deserved someone who was able to return her feelings, to love her completely—someone like him. Ephram knew he should be happy about this new piece of information. But Amy looked just as stricken right now as he imagined she must have felt at that moment four months ago.

Ephram loved her. How could he be happy about something that made her so miserable?

"Maybe . . . maybe he was just having a hard time with the words," he offered. "Sometimes people want to say things but they just can't."

"Maybe," she whispered. "Or maybe he never loved me. Either way, my last words to him were cold ones. And the worst part—worse than the waiting and the operation, and the tubes and the machines—sometimes I think he wasn't just going for a joyride that afternoon. I think he was running from me. Maybe if I hadn't scared him off . . ."

Now this Ephram could handle. This he knew from his own experience. This he could help her with—and he didn't have to be a cheerleader. He could be himself. "Amy, this sounds lame, but I know how you feel. For a long time after my mom had her accident, I was sure it was my fault. Blaming yourself is just a way to try to make sense of something that will never make sense. When the truth is, it was what it was: an accident."

Amy hung on his words, absorbing them. When he stopped talking, the hum of the fluorescent lights filled the silence. And slowly the haunted look left Amy's face.

"It's kind of amazing, isn't it?" she finally said. "Out of all the people I've known my whole life, you're the only one who showed up today."

Ephram was speechless. He'd never felt so raw as he did sitting there, staring at this incredible girl who could say things like that to him and still love someone else. How could he deal with that? What was he supposed to tell her?

Suddenly Amy's eyes left his. She took one look over his shoulder, then leaped out of her chair and ran across the empty cafeteria to where Dr. Brown stood in the doorway with Brian.

"How is he?" Amy blurted out.

"He's out of surgery," Andy said. "If you want to see him, Brian here will show you the way."

Amy took a few steps after Brian. Then she turned and ran back to throw her arms around Ephram's father. "Thank you, Dr. Brown," she said, kissing his cheek.

Grinning tiredly, Andy came over and sat down.

"Considering a career in neurosurgery?" he joked, nodding toward Amy.

"I am now," Ephram replied. "So how did it go?"

His dad shrugged. "Okay. I'm not sure we did any good. From here on in, it's wait and see."

"I meant how did it go for *you*?" Ephram asked. "First time back and all."

He could tell his father was trying to work up his usual breezy reply. But after a moment he gave up. "Truthfully?" he said. "I was scared."

Ephram nodded. His dad didn't know he'd overheard the conversation with Brian the night before. Still, it was nice to know that the Great Dr. Brown would admit his true feelings to his son.

"What were you scared of?" Ephram asked.

"That I would fail Colin. Amy. The Harts. You."

"You were scared you'd fail *me*?" Ephram hadn't been expecting that.

"Yeah, I was," his father said. "But the CD you made me helped. Bobby Short, inspired choice. And very New York."

"I'm glad you liked it," Ephram said. And he meant it.

CHAPTER 8

For a week, Colin slept. And Amy apparently
didn't. As far as Ephram could tell, she didn't
sleep, she didn't eat, and she didn't have a single
thought in her head that wasn't about Colin.

Ephram's father wasn't much better. He looked
like hell, he had insomnia, and he didn't eat. It
wasn't Colin he was worried about, though. He
didn't talk about it, but Ephram knew what he was
thinking: His parents' anniversary was the next day.
It would have been their twentieth. His father was
slipping back into the misery of the first few
months, and Ephram didn't know how to help him.

At least Delia didn't seem to notice. Their dad
put up a good front for her. At breakfast, he chatted
with Nina, who was going to drive Delia to school.
Ephram listened to the small talk without taking
much in. It was enough to know that his father

was starting out the day okay. At least he hadn't reverted to talking to Ephram's mom again.

When he finished eating, Ephram shoved back his chair and stood. He handed his father a permission slip he needed signed.

"What's this?" his dad asked.

"Field trip to a mine," Ephram told him.

"Sounds educational."

"Yes. What kind of future will I have without knowing how a mine operates?" Ephram said sarcastically. Nina smiled.

"Come on, Ephram," his dad said. "You don't want to be the only kid in your school who doesn't know where coal comes from, do you?"

There's the old clueless Dad, Ephram thought, cheering up a bit. "Silver, Dad," he said. "In Colorado it's silver."

"Silver?" His father looked surprised. "Huh."

Delia came in with her coat on and Nina stood up to go. With a kiss on the cheek, Delia was off to school, leaving Ephram alone with his father. It was time to say something about the anniversary. He couldn't just let it hang out there for his dad to deal with alone.

"Hey, Dad," he said casually. "You know, I don't *have* to go on this field trip."

"Why wouldn't you?"

"I don't know. I figured tomorrow . . . I know it's your anniversary."

His father forced a smile. "Don't worry about that. Your mother never liked to make a big deal out of our anniversary anyway."

"Since when?" Ephram challenged him. "Last year you guys flew off to Hawaii."

"Yeah, well. It was one of the smaller islands. We had a coupon."

Ephram rolled his eyes. He wasn't buying any of this. He knew exactly how much his mom had always loved celebrating their anniversary. He was usually the one who'd helped her plan it. In fact he knew that she'd been planning a trip to Italy for their twentieth. It was where they'd had their honeymoon. He raised his eyebrows and waited for his dad to stop pretending everything was okay.

His father held up his hands in surrender. "Your concern is appreciated, Ephram, but I'm fine. Now stop loitering. Get to school."

It sounded sincere, but Ephram wasn't sure whether to believe him or not. But there was no point in forcing the issue. He patted his dad on the back, grabbed his backpack, and headed out to school.

The next day—his parents' actual anniversary— Ephram again volunteered to stay home, but his father sent him off again. Ephram promised himself he'd make dinner really count as family time tonight.

By the time they got to the mine, Amy was completely out of it. She was even ignoring her friend Kayla. All her focus was concentrated on her cell phone as she waited for the call that would let her know Colin had regained consciousness.

"Hey, Ame, your phone won't work down here," Kayla said as the class entered the mine.

Amy just stared off into space, clutching the phone to her chest. Ephram could see by her expression that she was doing it again—picturing that moment when Colin woke up. When she could apologize to him, and he could tell her he loved her, and they could start their great romance all over again.

"Amy!" Kayla barked.

Amy jumped and looked at her. "Your phone won't work," Kayla repeated. "Don't waste the battery."

Amy stared at the phone as if it had betrayed her. "You're right, there's no service," she said. "I'm gonna run outside and see if there are any messages."

She took off without even bothering to make sure the teacher wasn't watching. Ephram thought about going after her to offer her his umbrella; a storm had been blowing up when they came down into the mine. But Amy was already gone, still cradling the cell. Wendell sidled up to Ephram.

"I bet you wish you were that phone, bro," he cracked.

"Shut up, Wendell," Ephram snapped.

Kayla looked disgusted. "God, I cannot wait for Colin to wake up already," she said. "Then everything will finally get back to normal around here."

"What's normal?" Ephram asked.

"Put it this way; Amy won't have you and I hanging out together anymore," she said.

It was what he'd expected to hear. But that didn't mean it felt good.

The mine was everything Ephram had expected it to be—cold, dark, dirty, and boring. Finally they were released into the gift shop up on the surface while Ms. Caleb, the science teacher, went out to make sure the bus was ready.

Ephram flipped through a rack of postcards featuring old black-and-white shots of Everwood from a century before. It looked basically the same.

"My mom has a bigger version of that in her office," Amy said, looking over his shoulder. "It's her favorite picture."

Ephram wanted to say something clever, but the smell of Amy's shampoo and the nearness of her took his breath away. It was the first non-mine-related thing she'd said to him all day.

"People, may I have your attention?" Ms. Caleb's voice cut through the chatter. "Route 79 has been closed due to the storm. It's pretty bad out there."

"Are we gonna have to sleep here?" Kayla demanded.

"No," the teacher answered. "But I'd like you all to contact your parents to tell them you'll be late. There are public phones in the hall."

Before she'd even finished speaking, kids were pushing past her to get to the phones. There were shrieks and general hysteria, as if they were going to be trapped in the mine for a week.

"This bites," Ephram said, almost to himself.

"Did you have plans?" Amy asked.

"Kinda," he said. "I was supposed to have dinner with my dad. It's his anniversary."

"Ouch. How's he handling it?"

Ephram didn't know how much to tell her. Was she really interested, or was she going to drift off into another Colin daydream any second? "Well, he's not talking to her like she's still here," he began. "I consider that a step in the right direction."

Amy gave him a sympathetic look. It seemed as if she really was paying attention, not just going through the motions while she thought about Colin. She opened her mouth to answer, but Todd, the idiot from Ephram's gym class, stepped in between them. He had two other idiots in tow, as usual.

"Yo, Amy," Todd said. "I can't deal with the masses. Can I borrow your phone?"

"Uh, it's not really working here," Amy said.

"I saw you talking on it like two minutes ago," Todd pointed out.

"Yeah, well, I'd like to keep the line open. I'm expecting an important call," Amy explained.

Todd rolled his eyes and turned away. "From Coma Boy? Like that's gonna happen," he joked to one of his idiot friends.

"Amy—," Ephram began, but she'd already turned away, stung. She was pretending to study the postcard rack, and Ephram could tell that she was barely holding it together. She clearly wanted to be alone, so he went and got in line for the pay phones.

When it was finally his turn, he dialed home. His dad answered on the first ring. "Ephram?" he said. "Where are you? I'm about to start cooking."

"I'm at the mine still."

"Still?"

"There's a storm so they're making us stay here until it passes," Ephram explained.

"Oh." Ephram could hear the disappointment in his father's voice. "Do you think it'll be long? Because I can hold dinner."

The truth was that Ephram had never wanted to eat his father's crappy cooking more. He knew Delia was staying over at Nina's tonight, which meant his dad would be all alone. But he didn't want to get his hopes up and then disappoint him even more.

"I think we're gonna be late," he said. "They said we won't be leaving until nine at the earliest."

"Oh. So you won't make it back for dinner."

Ephram turned his back to the line of kids waiting for the phone. "I'm sorry, Dad," he said.

"No, no, it's fine, it's just fine," his father said quickly.

"There's nothing I can do."

"Of course not. Ephram, don't worry. I'll see you when I see you."

"Dad—"

"Wake me up when you get home if I'm asleep, okay? Bye." His father hung up before Ephram could say another thing. Ephram placed the phone back into its cradle and stepped away to let the next person use it.

Things were easier when we ignored each other, he thought. Ephram sighed, thinking about the pain in his dad's voice just now. Ephram sighed. He could see the rain lashing against the windows of the hallway, and a brief flash of lightning lit the sky. It was a stormy night. *Just like the night Mom died,* he thought. And his father was alone in the storm, on his twentieth anniversary.

Ephram headed back into the gift shop. He'd noticed a leather bag hanging on the wall over the cashier, an old-fashioned doctor's bag. His dad had told him he needed to make a new home for himself in Everwood. Well, that was true for both of them. His dad wasn't the famous neurosurgeon married to the love of his life, not anymore. Now he was a widowed family doctor in a small town. He needed a doctor's bag. And he needed something to cheer him up.

The cashier had just given Ephram his change when he heard a cell phone ring. He whipped his head around to find Amy frantically searching for the phone in her purse. She finally found it, yanked it out, and hit talk.

"Hello?" she cried. "Hello . . . ? Yes, this is Amy Abbott."

That sounded official. Was it the hospital calling? Ephram could see the frantic hope in Amy's eyes. Well, first there was hope. Then the tiniest bit of confusion. "Who's this?" she asked.

Ephram glanced out the glass door of the gift shop into the hallway. Todd the idiot stood at the pay phone with his two buddies. All of them were laughing as Todd spoke into the phone.

"I'm calling to tell you that your boyfriend's doing very well. He's sitting up right now and singing the greatest hits of *Nsync," Todd said in a fake nasal voice.

Ephram heard Amy's outraged answer as he ran through the gift shop door, out into the hall, and straight into Todd. There wasn't a single thought in his head as he felt himself leap through the air to tackle the moron who was purposely hurting Amy.

They both crashed to the ground, Todd dropping the phone. "You think that's funny?" Ephram cried, picturing Amy's hopeful eyes. Picturing his father at home alone.

"Get off of me, jerk!" Todd yelled, scrambling to his feet. His two friends stepped closer, but Ephram barely noticed them. He launched himself at Todd again, this time pushing him back against the wall. "Do you ever think before you open your stupid mouth?" he hissed.

Todd shoved him away. "Who are you, the coma police?" he demanded.

"Are you really that much of a dumbass?" Ephram shouted. "Do you have any idea what it means to lose somebody?" He pulled back his arm, hand curled into a fist. He couldn't wait to smash that stupid look off Todd's face.

Ms. Caleb jumped in between them. "Stop it right now!" she cried. "Or you'll both be taking this class next semester!"

Ephram lowered his hand and took a step back, noticing for the first time that the entire class had spilled out into the hall to watch the fight. Amy stood in the doorway of the gift shop, staring at him.

Kayla approached her, but Amy just turned away and wandered off by herself. Ephram waited until everyone had gone back to doing whatever they were doing before his little outburst. Then he went in search of Amy.

He found her in one of the galleries that had been set up as a mining museum. She sat in an old mining car, staring off into space, alone in the dark—probably the way his dad was sitting alone right now. *Well, at least I can help one of them,* Ephram thought.

"Hey," he said.

Amy turned to him. He could tell she was trying to smile, but she couldn't quite manage it.

"I think this area's off-limits," he said.

"Let 'em arrest me."

"I'll show you how to take a mug shot," Ephram offered. "You can check out my seventh-grade school picture."

This time she did smile. A little. Ephram climbed into the mining car and sat next to her. Her cell phone lay on the seat in between them. Amy didn't say anything.

"Can you imagine working down here?" Ephram asked after a moment. He glanced around at the dank, blackish walls. "Spending whole days without ever seeing the sky."

"I feel like I've been *living* down here for the last four and a half months," Amy replied. "Every waking minute's been about trying to get back to the light, trying to turn back time. Convincing Colin's parents to let him have the surgery, convincing your dad that he was the only one to do it. And now the surgery's over, Colin's still lying in that bed, and I can't convince myself that any of it was worth it."

"It was," Ephram told her.

"No." She shook her head. "Even my friends look at me like I'm pathetic, because I'm waiting around, hoping for . . ."

"A miracle," Ephram finished for her. "You should. I hear they happen every once in a while."

Amy looked down at her hands and didn't answer. Ephram wasn't sure if he was helping or just making things worse. She'd obviously come here to be alone; maybe he should let her be alone. But he wanted to stay here, sitting with the girl he loved, even if his love didn't mean a thing to her. He might not have much more time to be with her like this. If she got her miracle, she'd forget all about him, just like Kayla said.

All of a sudden Ephram felt like he couldn't take it anymore. He'd been tiptoeing around the truth about their relationship ever since he met Amy. He wanted it out in the open.

"Can I ask you something?" he blurted out.

"Sure."

"If Colin suddenly woke up tomorrow, you and I . . . would we become total strangers?"

"Strangers?" She drew back a little as if he'd offended her. "Ephram, I've shared more with you in these last few months than I've ever shared with anybody in my life."

"Yeah, I know," he said, feeling stupid for asking and trying to backpedal. "But—"

"You're the only person who's been here for me this whole time. You came with me to the hospital. You helped me convince your dad. And the way you stood up for me back there? You're the person who's gotten me through this."

Wow, Ephram thought. *That was pretty much the perfect answer.* It was hard to believe that he was sitting here with Amy, actually hearing her say how much he meant to her. He couldn't take his eyes off her.

"The way I see it," Amy went on, "if there's any miracle in my life right now, it's the fact that your dad looked at a map, and of all places, decided to move here." She turned toward him suddenly, and their faces were inches apart.

Ephram's breath caught in his throat. He knew he was supposed to move away, or at least *look* away. But Amy's gaze didn't waver. She stared into his eyes as if willing him to understand how much she needed him.

He leaned forward, his body simply moving by itself. Amy's eyes closed, and their lips met. Time stopped, thoughts stopped, and Ephram's entire life was kissing Amy.

She pulled away, the cold air of the mine hitting him like a slap as her body's warmth vanished from his side. "We should probably check," she said in a rush, climbing out of the car. "They might be boarding already."

"Yeah, okay." Ephram's voice sounded shrill even to himself. Amy didn't look back as she hurried out of the gallery.

Ephram stayed put, alone in the dark. He felt like the biggest idiot on the planet.

By the time Ephram left the darkness of the gallery a half-hour later, the bus was boarding. He climbed slowly up the steps, trying not to be too obvious about the fact that he was searching for Amy.

He spotted her instantly, sitting by herself. Was she saving the seat for him? Should he go sit with her? After all, they'd kissed. She'd kissed him back, he was pretty sure. So that meant something. He didn't know exactly *what* it meant, but it was something. When you kiss a girl, you get to sit with her afterwards, right?

Their eyes met. Amy gave him a nervous smile.

Then she turned to Kayla, who was already sitting in the row across from her. "Kay!" Amy called, patting the seat next to her. Kayla got up and moved to Amy's seat, and Amy didn't look at Ephram again.

A burning feeling rose from Ephram's feet to his face. He felt humiliated. She'd completely blown him off. Had everyone seen that? Did they all know what had happened in the gallery?

He made his way to where Wendell was sitting and collapsed into the seat next to him, shell-shocked. How was it possible for a relationship to go from "you're the one who got me through this" to total ice in the space of a half-hour?

"Where've you been? I was starting to think Ms. Caleb threw you down a shaft," Wendell said conversationally.

Well, at least no one else knows what happened, Ephram thought. Because if anyone knew, it would be Wendell. But it was small comfort. Amy sat two rows behind him, but she might as well have been on Mars. Who needed Colin to ruin their friendship? Ephram had managed to do it all on his own.

Amy's cell phone rang. He heard her muffled "Hello?"

"Who is it?" Kayla demanded loudly.

"Hey, Dad. We're just about to leave," Amy was saying. Then her voice rose about an octave. "*What?* When?"

"What? What is it?" Kayla cried. "Is it about Colin?"

"He woke up," Amy said. "He's out of the coma."

"Dude," Wendell whispered, nudging Ephram's arm. "Did you just hear that?"

Ephram glared at him. What was he supposed to say? *Yes, I heard the final nail being hammered into the coffin of my friendship with Amy.* He ignored Wendell and plugged his headphones into his ears. Maybe it would drown out the sound of Amy's happiness.

CHAPTER 9

Ephram had been expecting things to be bad after Colin woke up, but he'd only had a vague idea what that meant. In his mind, it was a formless kind of bad—no specifics, just . . . not good. But now that it had actually happened, he was starting to learn exactly *how* it was bad.

It was bad because Amy had been practically sprinting up and down the aisle of the bus the whole way back from the mine. She couldn't wait to tell every single person who would listen all the details of Colin's waking moments. Every single person except Ephram, of course. She didn't even look at him.

It was bad because suddenly Ephram found himself treated like a normal human being by all the kids who'd been ignoring him since school started. Now that his father had pulled off another miracle, everyone was *pretending* to like Ephram. But his one real friend wasn't talking to him at all.

It was bad because after Colin woke up, the news broke that Bright had been the one driving the car when Colin was hurt. So every time Ephram saw Amy in town with her family, there seemed to be a giant wall of ice between her and her brother.

It was bad because Ephram's father told him that even with Colin awake, there was still a very long road to recovery, and a million obstacles to overcome.

But mostly it was bad because Ephram wanted to be able to talk to Amy about all of those things. He wanted to tell her he was sorry that she hadn't been there when Colin woke up. He wanted to tell her he shouldn't have kissed her down there in the mine. He wanted to tell her he was happy for her, because he was, sort of. He wanted to let her vent her feelings about her brother driving the car that almost killed her boyfriend. He wanted to tell her she could lean on him during Colin's long recovery.

But she wouldn't make eye contact, and she certainly wouldn't talk to him.

Everwood without Amy was cold and lonely and boring. The people who tried to be friends with Ephram now that his father had revived Colin disgusted him. His classmates in New York had never been this shallow.

Plus, his father's behavior had gotten worse again. When Ephram had given him the anniversary present he'd bought—the doctor's bag—he could tell his dad was touched by the gesture. Ephram felt as if they might be able to develop an actual relationship. For about two minutes, until Nonny and Grandpa Jacob showed up.

Ephram hadn't seen his mother's parents since the day he left New York. He'd talked to them, of course. But when he and Delia came downstairs one morning to find Nonny making their mother's special French toast, it was the best surprise he could imagine. And his father had totally ruined it. Ephram had barely even closed his door after breakfast when his dad opened it and stormed in.

"Did you know about this?" he demanded.

"About Grandpa and Nonny's trip? No." It was true. Ephram had known they were planning a visit. He could tell they were insulted that his father hadn't invited them yet. And maybe he'd even hinted to them that they should just come without waiting for an invitation. But he hadn't known they were coming *today*.

"Do me a favor while they're here," his father said. "You know how you usually behave?"

"Distant and miserable?" Ephram replied.

"Yeah. Do the opposite," his dad told him, shutting the door. Ephram felt a burst of the old, familiar anger. Nonny and Grandpa were the closest thing to his mother he had left. If they didn't like how he behaved toward his father, they'd blame his father, not him. And that was perfectly fine with Ephram.

He was even more annoyed than usual when he got to school that day. It was bad enough having to go to school at all lately, but having to leave his grandparents behind at home just made it all worse. He wished he could spend the day touring Everwood with them the way Delia was, but his father had forbidden it. Somehow it was more important that Ephram be here, feeling miserable, than being happy hanging out with Grandpa Jacob.

He was locking his bike to the rack when he spotted Amy getting out of her dad's car. She had a big camping backpack and a giant duffel bag. There was no way she could carry them both. Ephram took a deep breath and went over to talk to her.

"Need help?" he asked.

"That's okay, I got it." She dragged the duffel another few feet toward the school, breathing hard with the effort.

"So are you breaking your back right now for the feminist movement?" Ephram asked. "Or because you don't want to walk with me? Because I can respect both."

"Why wouldn't I want to walk with you?" Amy asked, as if the answer weren't the most obvious thing on earth.

"I dunno," Ephram said. "The whole mine thing?"

"That was an accident. Let's just forget about it, okay?" Amy said quickly. "And the bag really isn't that heavy. It's just clothes and stuff for the weekend. I'm going straight to the hospital after school today."

Ephram was still stuck on the part about their kiss being an accident. *Is that possible?* He thought. *Could you really kiss someone accidentally?* "Uh . . . so you're staying over in Denver?" he asked.

"I'm pretty much gonna be there every weekend until Colin comes home. He really needs me right now," she said.

Ephram knew what *that* meant: *I have a boyfriend, so how about you stop kissing me in mines?* He adopted a more lighthearted tone of voice. "So I guess you won't be going to that bonfire party tomorrow night."

"No can do," Amy said.

"That's too bad. It sounds kinda cool." Ephram was just babbling now, trying to convince her that the mine thing was no big deal. "I've never partied in a canyon before. New Yorkers, we're more basement people."

"Hey, just 'cause I'm not going doesn't mean you shouldn't go," Amy pointed out.

"Yeah, I know that," Ephram said quickly. This really wasn't going well. The bell rang, mercifully cutting short their time together. Amy hurried off, yanking her giant duffel after her. He didn't see her again for the rest of the day.

Luckily Grandpa and Nonny had come to Everwood and were making him feel better, even though he had to put up with his father being rude to them. The Great Dr. Brown didn't even make it home from work until after eight o'clock, and when he finally arrived, he totally lied to Grandpa about Ephram's piano lessons. Ephram and his dad had never even talked about him taking piano lessons, but his father wanted him to tell Grandpa Jacob that they were still looking for the right teacher. Ephram was happy to see that his grandfather saw right through the whole thing. Having them around was the closest thing to having his mother around again, running interference between Ephram and his father.

The next morning, after a pathetic attempt at making breakfast, Ephram's dad announced that they were all going to the annual Father-Son Flyfest, which apparently was some kind of Everwood torture session involving fly-fishing. Ephram turned him down. He wasn't about to pretend that they did generational-bonding things like this just to impress Grandpa.

But then his grandfather surprised him by wanting to do the fly-fishing thing. It still sounded like a nightmare to Ephram, but he couldn't exactly say no to Grandpa Jacob. On the way out, the Great

Dr. Brown bailed on them to go visit a patient. So all in all, things could've been worse. At least he wouldn't have to spend the day standing in a river with his know-it-all dad.

Somehow Grandpa Jacob knew how to fly-fish. Ephram didn't know how the guy managed to be a top-notch surgeon, an attentive grandfather, *and* a fly-fishing mentor. In his entire life, he'd never come across anything that Grandpa Jacob couldn't do.

"This place is amazing," Ephram's grandfather said, looking around at the Larchmont River. A row of fathers and sons stood in twos, all of them ready to cast. Grandpa Jacob gazed at the mountains, the clear blue sky, the crystalline water. "I can't believe your dad never took you out here before."

"Fishing's not really our thing," Ephram said.

"Not even the 'new Andy'?" his grandfather joked. "The furry, PTA, waffle-making Andy?"

Ephram grinned. His dad's new beard was pretty bizarre. But other than that, it didn't seem to Ephram that the guy had changed all that much. Like now, for instance, he was off with a patient instead of here bonding with his son. That wasn't any different from the old Andy.

The sound of creaking rubber caught his attention, and he looked up to see Bright with Dr. Abbott. Bright's hip-waders were obviously new, and clearly the cause of the ridiculous sound.

"Hey, freakazoid," Bright greeted him. "I didn't know you did sunlight."

"I didn't know you moonlighted as a condom," Ephram replied, gesturing to Bright's ugly boots.

Luckily, Bright and his father kept walking downstream to set up. Having to deal with him could very well ruin Ephram's day.

For a few hours, everything was perfect—except for Ephram's fishing skills, which failed to improve despite Grandpa Jacob's guidance. But otherwise, the day was great—beautiful, crisp late-autumn weather, his grandfather to talk to, and for once nobody gossiping about Colin Hart.

Then Bright approached him. For a while as he squeaked toward them, Ephram figured Bright was just going back up to his car for something. No such luck. He stopped right next to Ephram. "I gotta talk to you about something," he announced.

"You got the results back from your IQ test and you failed?" Ephram asked.

"It's about Amy," Bright said, not even bothering to play the insult game. "You gotta come to Sean's party tonight. The one in the canyon—"

"Forget it," Ephram interrupted. "I already know she's not gonna be there, so don't bother." He couldn't believe Bright was still trying to play tricks on him, even after all that had happened between him and Amy.

"You don't know anything," Bright snapped. "Amy's

on her way back from Denver right now. Colin's folks don't want her hanging around the hospital anymore, and she's, like, completely depressed."

There was a look in Bright's eyes that Ephram had never seen before. It was serious, and a little bit frightened. Ephram studied his bland, simple face for a moment. Amy was barely even speaking to her brother these days, so for Bright to be worried about her . . . well, she had to be pretty seriously messed up.

"What do you mean?" he asked. "Why don't they want her there?"

"I don't know. I guess she's stressing everyone out," Bright said. "Colin still doesn't remember who anyone is, so—"

"Whoa," Ephram said, shocked. "What do you mean he doesn't remember?"

"What are you, my echo or something?" Bright sneered. "I'm telling you, it's bad. So I'm bringing her to the party tonight and you're gonna be there to cheer her up."

"Why would me being there cheer her up?" Ephram asked.

"Believe me, I don't get it any more than you do. But for some reason you're the only person who makes my sister smile."

Ephram couldn't help smiling himself when he heard that. He would definitely be at that party.

• • •

"You're not going," Andy said.

The Great Dr. Brown had some stupid idea that he could jump in on the father-son bonding thing by taking Ephram and Grandpa Jacob out to dinner. Apparently it didn't matter that he'd totally bailed on them earlier.

"You can either sit in your room or come to dinner with your grandfather and me. Your choice," his father finished.

There were a million replies Ephram wanted to give, but nothing he said was ever going to get through his father's thick skull. There was no point in arguing. He turned and stomped up to his room.

He could hear his dad and Grandpa Jacob fighting downstairs. He knew they were fighting about him, but he didn't care. All he could think about was getting to that party—and to Amy. If Colin was really as bad as Bright said, she must be freaking out. And for the Harts to tell her to stay away . . . well, she must be freaking out big-time. He had to be there for her.

Ephram went over to his stereo and turned it up loud. Then he grabbed his jacket and headed for the window. He'd never climbed out a window before. It wasn't something you did much when you lived on the fifty-third floor of a high rise in Manhattan. But suburban kids always did on TV. How hard could it be?

There was a ledge about six feet below his window that he decided he could probably jump down to. The loud music would cover the sound. Taking a deep breath, he jumped to the ledge.

It was more slippery than he was expecting. He slid almost to the edge. Catching himself, he peered over, judging the distance to the ground. At least eight feet. "I'm going to die for a kegger," he muttered. "Genius."

He closed his eyes and jumped. The ground was hard, and he landed on his knees, banging them up pretty good. "Alrighty then," he said. The escape was harder than he'd expected. He limped off toward his bike. It was going to be a long night.

The party was bigger than he thought it would be. Lots of the people there didn't even go to County High. The place basically consisted of a bunch of SUVs and pickups parked in a group, headlights on. Someone had a boombox blasting music, and there was a long line snaking through the party to the keg. Most people were just hanging around in little groups or making out in the cars. Some were dancing.

Amy was sitting by herself on the hood of a truck, looking as out of place as Ephram felt. "This hood taken?" he asked. She patted the place next to her and he climbed up onto the truck. "I think I saw an actual coyote waiting in line for the keg," he joked.

She smiled, and Ephram's heart did a little leap. Maybe Bright was right about him. Maybe he was the only one who could make her smile.

"I thought you couldn't make it," she commented.

"I was gonna say the same to you."

"Bright practically shoved me into his car. I didn't have much choice."

"Well, you look nice. For someone who was forcibly removed from their home and all." Ephram didn't get to see if Amy smiled that time, because a big jock stepped up, blocking out all the light. "Tequila, anyone?" he asked, waving around a bottle and a stack of Dixie cups. "I'll show you how to do a body shot, Amy," he added with a leer.

"I'll pass," she said dryly.

The jock turned to Ephram. "New Dude?" he asked, waving the bottle.

"I'm good, thanks," Ephram replied. The guy walked off and Ephram glanced over at Amy. She gave him a small smile. He moved a little closer to her. "So how are you really?" he asked.

"I'm fine. I'm good."

She was lying. He decided to press her a little. After all, she clearly needed someone to talk to. "I heard Colin was . . . that he's not doing too great?"

Amy's nostrils flared. She spun to face Ephram, looking as if she might slap him. "Actually, he's doing amazing," she snapped.

"Oh." Ephram wasn't sure what to do. Somehow he'd made her angry. He tried to remember what his dad had told him about Colin's recovery. "'Cause I know sometimes it takes a while for people to fully recuperate after head traumas and stuff."

"How would you know that?" Amy challenged him. "Have you ever known anyone who's been in a coma?"

"I asked my dad," he explained. "I know that the progress is slow. Sometimes it's even harder on the people who are waiting for the person to get better, you know?"

"Why are you telling me all this?" Amy demanded. "I didn't ask you to, Ephram."

How did this conversation go so horribly wrong? Ephram thought as he fumbled for an answer. "I just see you so stressed out all the time and I want to help."

"You can't."

"I'm sure you're fine, Amy," he said gently. "I just think maybe you should take a break. You know? Until he's back in school again. Try to move on a little bit."

Ephram stopped talking. Amy's face had turned into a mask of fury. He'd never seen her look so cold. "You know what, Ephram?" she said. "Maybe *you* should move on."

She jumped the hood and stalked off into the

crowd, leaving Ephram speechless. Move on. He should move on . . . from her? Is that what she really wanted? Is that the thanks he got for trying to help her deal with her bedridden boyfriend for all these months?

The jock made his way back by the truck, still offering tequila shots. Ephram waved to him. "I'll have one of those," he said. *In fact,* he thought, *maybe I'll have two.*

Ephram was pretty drunk by the time the cops got there. So drunk that they caught him peeing on a bush, which wasn't nearly as embarrassing as Ephram expected. *I guess that's what being drunk means,* he thought as a police officer led him to one of the cop cars. *Means you don't care about public urination. Or Amy telling you to move on.* He giggled a little bit. He'd been amusing himself with his own cleverness all night. He didn't even need an audience; he just talked to himself.

His father didn't look very amused when he opened the front door. One look at his baffled, furious face was enough to ruin Ephram's good mood.

"Is this your son?" the police officer who'd brought him home asked.

"Can't be," Ephram's father replied. "My son is safely tucked into his bed upstairs." Ephram rolled his eyes. His dad always had to be a drama queen.

"He's not Ephram Brown?" the officer asked, clearly having no concept of sarcasm.

"That depends. What did he do?"

"Public intoxication, underage drinking. He's never been a problem before so we didn't take him in. But if we catch him again . . . "

"If you catch him again you better keep him," Andy said menacingly. "Thank you, officer."

As the cop left, Ephram tried to go straight upstairs. His father grabbed his arm. "You gotta be kidding me," he growled. "Are you drunk?"

"Not enough," Ephram joked. "But we can correct that. Toss me a Heineken."

"You think this is funny?" his father said. "It's bad enough you drank—and don't think we aren't going to talk about that—but you have to pick this weekend to turn into a teenager? You haven't been to a party since we got here. All of a sudden you're getting plastered and arrested? If you wanted to embarrass me in front of your grandparents, you've done a real good job."

Ephram jerked his arm away. "That's exactly what I'm doing," he snapped. "It's all about *you*. I got arrested just so *you* could feel bad about yourself."

"That's not what I meant."

"It's not?" Ephram put on a fake Dr. Brown voice. "'Look at me, I'm Super Dad. Let's fish and make waffles.'" He leaned in to whisper in his dad's ear. "I got bad news. They're not falling for it. But if you raise my allowance, I promise I'll hug you tomorrow. Right in front of Grandpa."

Ephram felt pretty proud of that one as he walked upstairs to his room. But he knew the guilt would set in soon.

The next morning was hell. He'd never had a hangover before, and it was just as bad as everyone said. Plus for some perverse reason his grandfather had decided to drag him along on a grocery-store trip first thing in the morning. Ephram thought the bright fluorescent lights and Muzak might just kill him. Finally Grandpa Jacob got to the point.

"You did a stupid thing last night," he said.

"He was being unreasonable," Ephram muttered.

"I'm not arguing that. But sneaking out, getting drunk, that's for children. You're not a child, Ephram."

"He treats me like one."

"So don't let him," Grandpa Jacob said. "When I was your age, we had no money, my family. I had to work every day after school just to help put food on the table. You grow up pretty fast that way. By the time I was sixteen, I was considered a man by my parents. The greatest gift they ever gave me. And you know what I found out?"

"What?"

"Getting what you want is easy. It's *knowing*

what you want that's the challenge. What do you want, Ephram? And I don't mean being able to go to a party. I mean in your life, right now, what do you wish for?"

Amy. The word popped into his mind instantly. But not just Amy. What did he wish for? For Amy not to be in love with Colin. For Colin not to have gotten hurt. For his father to be more like the person he seemed to be turning into before Nonny and Grandpa came to town. For his mother to still be alive.

Everything he wished for was impossible. "I don't know," Ephram answered.

"Well, figure it out," his grandfather told him. "Then make it happen."

It can't happen, Ephram thought sadly. None of it could happen. But maybe that's what his grandfather meant. Maybe he was supposed to figure out what he wanted that *could* happen. Maybe he was supposed to stop pining away for things that were finished, and start paying attention to things the way they actually were.

The shopping cart he was pushing slammed into another cart, the sound making Ephram's head pound again. He started to apologize, then saw that the person he'd collided with was Amy. She looked as embarrassed as he felt. But she immediately put on a fake smile. "Hey, Ephram. Is this your grandpa?" she asked, as if nothing

195

had happened between them the night before.

She was good at that, he realized. She was good at just ignoring the bad stuff.

Ephram wasn't.

"Grandpa, this is Amy Abbott," he muttered, not trying to hide his discomfort.

"Nice to meet you, Amy." Grandpa Jacob looked at him knowingly. "I'll go get you some aspirin," he said, leaving Ephram alone with Amy.

"So I heard the cops busted up the party last night," she said.

"Yup."

"Were you there when it happened?" she asked. "How long did you stay?" She was talking as though they were still just regular friends—as if she hadn't said the worst thing in the world to him last night. Did she really think pretending it didn't happen would make it go away? Ephram felt a surge of anger at her. He'd been a good friend to her even when it killed him to know she loved someone else. But she wasn't being a good friend to him. She wasn't even being honest with him.

"I stayed long enough to move on," he said pointedly.

He saw her face begin to crumble, so he turned and pushed his cart away. Even when he was mad at Amy he couldn't stand knowing he'd hurt her.

By the time he caught up with Grandpa Jacob, he

knew what it was that he wanted. He wanted his old life back. His old school, his old friends, his old piano teacher, and his old home. New York. Where he knew the rules, and where people didn't lie to him or jerk him around emotionally. Where maybe he could just concentrate on getting over his mother's death without having to worry about everyone else's problems, too. Delia's. Amy's. His father's. It wouldn't be the same without his mother. But if he could live with Nonny and Grandpa Jacob, it would almost be like having her around.

Even though his grandfather had said getting what he wanted was the easy part, Ephram was still surprised by his dad's reaction to the news—he just shrugged. Ephram and Grandpa Jacob had talked through the idea, and Grandpa and Nonny were thrilled to have Ephram come and live with them in New York. Grandpa Jacob had even offered to be there with Ephram when he told his dad. Clearly, they'd both been expecting a big scene.

But when Ephram said it had been his own idea to move back to New York, Andy just looked at him and said, "I see."

After Ephram went to bed, he could hear his father and grandfather's angry voices rising from downstairs. Clearly the discussion of his moving back to New York was not yet finished.

The next morning, Andy acted like there was

nothing wrong. Ephram wasn't sure whether to talk to his dad about New York or not. But since his father didn't bring it up, he didn't either.

Grandpa Jacob did, though. When he joined Ephram and his father in the kitchen, he'd already called Ephram's old school to make sure they would take him back.

"You could start up again as soon as winter term," Grandpa Jacob told him.

Ephram was shocked. "That's in like three weeks." Somehow he'd been thinking of this whole move-back-to-New-York thing as being in the distant future.

"We'd have to get you back before, of course," his grandfather said. "Give you time to get yourself together."

Ephram shot a glance at his father. He didn't look happy, but he wasn't saying anything.

"I forgot the best part," Grandpa Jacob went on. "The headmaster said, given the circumstances, he'll overlook your poor grades. Get your GPA back up and they'll forgive your whole time in Everwood."

"Cool," Ephram said. That seemed to be what his grandfather expected him to say. But it was a little weird to hear it out loud: When he went back home, his whole time in Everwood would be erased, forgotten, like it never happened. But it wouldn't really feel that way, would it? He couldn't imagine just forgetting about everything that had happened in the last few months. About Amy.

"That doesn't mean you don't have to go to school today," his father said.

Ephram didn't bother to answer. He just went upstairs to get ready. Obviously his father didn't care if he moved back to New York or not. Now the Great Doctor Brown had an excuse to be as curt and unfeeling with Ephram as he wanted to be. *No problem,* Ephram thought. *It'll be just like old times.*

After school, Nonny came into Ephram's room with a big smile on her face. "I finally found your mother's good napkins," she said. "Still in a box in the garage."

It took him a moment to remember what she was talking about. Delia and Nonny were planning a big formal birthday party for Edna the next night. They'd been cleaning the house, ordering food, and making all sorts of plans for days now. Ephram had been so wrapped up in his own plans that he'd barely even noticed.

"You on the phone?" Nonny asked, nodding at the cordless in Ephram's hand. He looked down, surprised to see it there. He'd been wondering whether or not to call Amy and tell her he was leaving, but he hadn't even realized that he'd picked up the phone.

"Not yet," he said to Nonny. "I'm trying to decide if I should tell anyone I might be moving."

"Like Delia."

Delia. Ephram hadn't even thought about how this might affect her. In fact he was beginning to realize that he hadn't thought through much about this move.

"She's a smart girl. She'll understand," said Nonny. "Maybe your father could help you talk to her."

He snorted. "He and I haven't exactly planned this out together. We haven't been talking much lately."

"Maybe you should."

"He seems pretty pissed," Ephram said.

"He is," Nonny agreed. "But not at you. Come with me." She led Ephram downstairs to the dining room and gestured at the gigantic round table. "This used to be our table," she said with a wistful smile. "Did anyone ever tell you about the first time your father and grandfather met?"

Ephram grinned, imagining the scene that must've been. It was no secret that they didn't like each other. "Was there much blood?" he joked.

"Jacob had been hearing it in both ears about your father for weeks—at the hospital about the genius hotshot and at home about this handsome kid sweeping Julia off her feet. And he doesn't like any of it. Well, she finally brings Andy home, we finish dinner, and your father has that look in his eye, like he knows what he wants and he's here to ask for it: permission to marry her."

"*That's* gonna go well," Ephram put in.

"So I shuffle Julia out of the dining room and leave them alone. Before your father gets out a word, Jacob pulls out this bottle of Polish vodka, the stuff his father used to drink. He puts the bottle down right here." She thumped the wooden table. "He takes out two shot glasses and starts pouring. One. They drink. Two, then four . . . Andy's eyes are glazing and Jacob is just getting warmed up. Those two went shot for shot for an hour, waiting to see which one would blink or drop first. Neither did. I'd never seen anyone keep up with Jacob before, but your father just wouldn't be beaten."

"He didn't want to lose?" Ephram asked.

"He didn't know how."

Ephram nodded. His father hadn't changed since then. "What happened?"

"They both fell asleep at the table," Nonny said with a smile. "Andy never did ask directly, and Jacob never did say yes directly. But as my father used to tell me, the Talmud says that silence is approval." She patted his hand. "Your father's not angry at you. It's been like this between them for years—they'll always be trying to drink each other under the table."

Ephram nodded, getting it. His father wasn't talking to him about New York because he didn't have any objections to the plan. Silence was approval. And that was good, right? Ephram wanted to go back home. There was nothing here for him now. The only thing that had ever made life in Everwood worth living was Amy, and they were barely even speaking. So he'd go to New York, and his father would go on living here with Delia. Somehow it would all work out. So why wasn't he happier?

It started snowing the next afternoon. Ephram just stayed in his room, avoiding all the catering people and the last-minute party preparations. It hadn't occurred to him until that morning that Amy would be coming to the party. After all, Edna was her grandmother. The entire Abbott family would have to be here. So Ephram took a little extra care with his hair. And he put on the suit that he knew he looked good in. He was attempting to knot his tie when his father came in.

"Someone just called for you from New York," Andy said. "You have a friend named Scug?"

"Yeah, remember? The guy who shaves his head." One look at his dad's face made it clear that he didn't remember. "He was only at the house like every day," Ephram muttered. The stupid tie was too short. He started over.

"Well he called. Said to tell you Kara Imm's planning a 'mondo' roof party before winter term. Apparently she is, let me make sure I have this right, 'totally hot for your ass.'"

Ephram chuckled. "City girls are a little faster than the girls out here." He thought about Kara Imm. She couldn't compete with Amy. Glancing down, he saw that he'd bungled his tie again. This time it was too long. He untied it.

"Look, Ephram," his dad said. "I want to talk to you about the New York thing."

"Can we do this later?" Ephram asked. "I need to get dressed."

Without a word, his father left. Ephram sighed in relief. Why bother talking about New York? He was going. What else was left to say?

Outside, the snow was falling harder. And inside, the party had started. Ephram knew he couldn't avoid Amy all night. He saw her when she arrived, but he just turned and walked away. After about an hour, he bumped into her on the stairs. She gave him an awkward smile. "Bathroom?"

"Up to the left," he said. "Past the very messy room." He tried to move past her, but Amy kept talking.

"You guys have a nice house, messy room notwithstanding."

Ephram sighed. She was trying to make things normal between them. It was hard to stay mad at

203

her when she was making such an effort. He figured he should at least be civil. He spotted Bright downstairs sitting on a couch, looking pale. "I'm glad the brain trust could come," he said.

"Relax. Bright'll be on his best behavior," Amy said, her voice becoming animated now that Ephram was actually talking to her. "He and Gramma aren't too great a couple. Bright wasn't the most adventurous kid and Gramma never had much patience for the skittish. I loved doing stuff with her, off-roading, wheelies. But Bright, let's just say she had to re-upholster the sidecar a few times."

Ephram couldn't help smiling at her speed-talking, but it still felt wrong to be acting as if nothing had happened between them. "Let's hope he's housebroken by now," he said, nodding at Bright. He started downstairs again.

"This is weird, huh?" Amy asked suddenly. He glanced at her in surprise—was she actually trying to be honest with him? "Look, you're stuck with me until cake," she went on. "We can hang up the tension if you want. Peace?"

Luckily he didn't have time to answer her. Grandpa Jacob bellowed at him from downstairs at the piano. "Ephram! Come show off for your guests!"

"Sorry, summoned," he told Amy, stepping past her.

"Hey—"

"It's fine. Peace," he said, not looking at her.

To Ephram's surprise, the party was actually kind of fun. Everyone he'd ever met in Everwood was there, and he was playing jazz tunes on the piano with his grandfather, and the snow was piling up on the window frames, making the firelit room seem cozy. Sure, Bright looked ready to puke. And Edna seemed miserable, even though it was her birthday. And he couldn't look at Amy. But otherwise, it was a good party.

Until Ephram was restacking a tray of blinis and his father was trying to get into the fridge for cheese, and they ended up walking right into each other.

"I'll get out of your way," Ephram offered.

"You don't have to. You could just sit still and talk to me for a minute," his dad said.

"How much talking is there to do?" Ephram asked, annoyed. His father was acting as if Ephram were the one who'd been purposely *not* talking these last few days. "I thought you'd be glad I was going."

"Thrilled, I already have plans to turn your room into a tennis court," his dad said. "Why would you think that?"

"Years of experience," Ephram replied.

"Forget me for a second. Have you even thought what this would do to your sister?" Andy asked.

That was low, Ephram thought. How dare he
drag Delia into this? "I've thought more about it
than you did before you moved us to this wasteland.
We'd have been fine if we just stayed in New York.
You'd be respectable and out of my face instead of
the town crazy." He pushed past his father. "I'm
going back."

"Just because you and your grandfather made up
your minds doesn't mean I have," Andy said. "I
may not be your favorite, but I'm still your father
and it's still my decision."

Ephram stopped in his tracks. He could see the
dining-room table through the door—the table
where the Great Dr. Brown had started his lifelong
competition with Grandpa Jacob. Everything Nonny
had told him suddenly made sense. He whirled to
face his father.

"Unbelievable. You're not even sorry I'm going,"
he spat. "You're just mad that I'm going with *him*.
It really is all a competition with you."

"You have no idea what this is to me. We can finish talking about this after you've calmed down."
Brushing past Ephram, his father walked right out
of the kitchen. As if the discussion were over. But
Ephram was furious, and not about to drop it. He
took off after his dad, making his way into the living room.

"Hey, if you want to talk, let's talk," he snapped.
His father glanced around at all their guests.

"Maybe we don't have to do this right now."

Ephram knew he was making a scene, but he didn't care. Soon enough he'd be gone anyway. Why should he care what anybody thought? "You know I miss home," he told his father. "Knowing my way around, having friends I can trust, not feeling like a freak all the time. I miss being around people who don't think *Cats* is an opera. All you have to do is say it. 'You can go to New York.' Just say it. You know you want to."

"Don't put words in my mouth," his dad replied, voice rising. "You're the one who asked to move back."

"You're leaving?" Delia cried. Ephram hadn't realized she was sitting on the couch, her eyes big and shocked. But there was nothing he could do about it now.

"No, honey," his dad told her. "He's only thinking about it."

"Come on, you love this stuff," Ephram said to his father. "My fate's in your hands. You didn't just drag me to live out here. You get to own me going back, too."

His father looked pale and overwhelmed. Ephram kind of liked knowing he could get that kind of reaction. "Really, I'm asking," he went on. "You tell me. Would I really be happier in Everwood? Or do you think I'd be better off in New York?"

Ephram waited. Everyone in the room waited.

His father's eyes never left his face. "I think you'd be happier if you went," said Andy.

It felt like a punch in the gut. That was the most surprising part to Ephram. His father had given him the answer he wanted, but it still felt like rejection. "That's what I thought," he said coldly.

Ephram just went back to the piano and played some more, instead of giving his father the satisfaction of seeing him storm off and hide in his room all night. Before long, people started talking again, probably gossiping about the unhappy Brown family. Ephram lost himself in the music, drowning out everything else. He didn't even notice when Delia came to sit on the bench beside him. At the end of his song, she looked up at him.

"Why do you and Dad hate each other?" she asked.

"We don't hate each other," he said. He realized that he didn't sound very convincing.

"Then how come you want to leave?"

"It's hard to explain." Delia just waited expectantly. "Remember last week when it was really cold and you tried on all your old sweaters from last winter?" he asked.

"I got too big for them."

"Right."

"I couldn't move my arms."

"That's kind of how I feel about Everwood," he said. "Does that make sense?"

"I think so. Except you're not too big. You fit here."

Ephram sighed. Delia was never going to understand why he wanted to leave. He wasn't even sure he understood anymore.

The snow had turned into a blizzard, and before long it was pretty clear that all of their guests would be spending the night. They'd begun napping on couches and chairs, and Bright was up in Delia's bedroom because he was sick. Ephram's father and his grandparents seemed kind of freaked out by the whole thing, but Ephram didn't mind. He sat outside on the back porch swing, staring up at the falling snow. It was amazing how something so gentle and pretty could create such havoc.

Amy stepped outside, a blanket wrapped around her shoulders. "You hiding?"

"Watching the snow," he replied. "It's different here. Chunkier. I used to like rain better, but now I'm on the fence."

"I like the snow," she said. "When it comes down like this, it's like time stops. And everyone's forced to stay home and . . . I dunno, drink hot chocolate. Am I allowed?" She gestured toward the swing.

Ephram brushed off a patch of snow and she sat down next to him. "Why didn't you tell me you were thinking of leaving?" she asked.

"I didn't think you'd have much of an opinion," he told her.

"Of course I would."

"That came out wrong," he said. He hesitated. He'd been angry at her for a while, but now that he was leaving it just seemed pointless to hold some kind of grudge against her. He might as well be honest. "I didn't tell you because I needed to decide for myself. You tend to have an effect on my moods."

"I've seen your moods. That's a lot of pressure."

"It's nothing you do on purpose, but when you're nice to me there's little I can't do. And when you're mad at me it's all I can think about," Ephram tried to explain. "And when I see something beautiful I only want to show it to you. And when you say things like 'You should move on,' it kinda stays with me for a while. You're in my head."

"Sorry," Amy said.

"It's not your fault."

"It is sometimes," she admitted. "I don't exactly have a history of being cautious with your feelings. If it helps, my mood's been lousy too. I thought it was bad when Colin was gone. Now he's awake and I can't even see him. His parents kicked me out, told me he's not ready. Well *I* am. And I am not a patient person."

"That bites," Ephram said.

"It really does. Anyway. Now that the decision's yours, you're really going?"

"I think so, yeah. New York has everything."

"Everwood has really good snow," Amy said.

He looked at her. "That's your pitch?" he asked. He wanted more. He'd just poured his heart out to her, and he wanted something in return. His father hadn't given him a reason to stay here. If anyone could, it was Amy.

She just shrugged sadly.

Okay, I guess that's it, Ephram thought. *Dad doesn't want me to stay, and neither does Amy.* He'd thought he would be happy to go back to New York. For some reason though, he wasn't.

There was a sudden commotion inside, and Ephram heard his father bellowing his name. With a final glance at Amy, he ran into the house and up to Delia's room. All three doctors—his father, his grandfather, and Dr. Abbott—were crowded around Bright, who lay on Delia's bed looking as white as the snow outside.

Shocked, Ephram glanced at Edna. "His appendix burst," she told him, her voice frightened. "Irv's going to try to get us to your dad's office in the truck."

"Ephram, get my toolbox," his father ordered him. "Put it on the dining-room table."

Ephram ran downstairs and within minutes he and his dad were sawing through the middle of his grandparents' old table to make a stretcher for Bright. As the table fell apart, Ephram couldn't help thinking that maybe it was a good time to get rid of that thing anyway. That table had too much bad history.

Once all the doctors had gone to Dr. Brown's office in town to take care of Bright, Ephram helped Nonny clean up the house and find everyone a place to sleep. He felt as if the snowstorm had put everything on hold for a little while—his fight with his dad, his anger at Amy, his decision to move to New York. Amy was right. The snow did stop time, or at least it seemed to give everyone a moment to catch their breath.

Delia was fast asleep on one of the kitchen chairs. Ephram scooped her up and carried her up to her bed. Ephram settled his little sister, then he lay down on the other side of the bed and closed his eyes. It was kind of nice, having all these people sleeping over in their house. It made the place feel like home.

Andy didn't get home until the last of the overnight guests were leaving the next morning. The city snow plows had come by about an hour earlier, and once the roads were cleared, Ephram had helped everyone dig out their cars to go. He was doing the remaining dishes when his father walked in looking exhausted.

"Mrs. Abbott called from the hospital. She said Bright got there okay," he told his dad.

"Good."

"You look beat up," Ephram commented. He knew his father had been the one to perform the emergency appendectomy on Bright last night. "How was Dr. Abbott?"

"He's a good dad. You could see if anything happened, he wouldn't survive it." Ephram's father gazed at him, his dark eyes serious. "I'm sorry, Ephram. I shouldn't have fought with you like that, with everyone there."

That was it. No excuses, no placing blame. Just an apology. Ephram wasn't sure he'd ever heard such a thing from his dad before. "It was my fault too," he admitted.

"But I'm supposed to be the grown-up around here, not you."

"It's fine," Ephram said.

"It's not fine," his father replied. "I do the wrong thing, I say the wrong thing, I say *awful* things. But I get so angry sometimes—"

"Yeah, I know," Ephram muttered.

"Not at you," his dad said. "I get angry at myself. Because I just can't get you to understand just how much I need you. When your mom died a thousand people told me a thousand stupid things, and I just wanted one of them to give me a good reason not to die. Then one night we were sitting there trying to eat and you just said, 'Everything's gonna be okay.' Nothing more. That was the first night I slept."

213

Ephram slowly sat down at the kitchen table. His father had never spoken to him like he was an adult before.

"You're the only one who can tell me everything will be okay and I believe it. I don't know why you're that person for me and I don't know why we don't treat each other better. I wish I could be the same for you." His father sat down too, looking defeated. "Instead you're miserable here, which is my fault, and if you go back to New York that might change. You'll probably be happier, I meant that. But I don't care. I want you to stay. I *need* you to stay."

Ephram tried to swallow down the lump in his throat. "Then I'll stay," he said.

Ephram was at Mama Joy's when Amy tracked him down the next day. He had gone there mostly just to get out of the house. Snowed in for one day was nice; snowed in for any more than that got oppressive. He wasn't expecting company. He certainly wasn't expecting Amy, since he still wasn't sure where they stood.

But there she was, taking a seat next to him at the counter. She spun around on her stool like a little girl, and Ephram felt himself fall in love with her all over again. Then, turning serious, she looked him straight in the eye.

"I got in a fight with Colin and he ended up in a

coma," she said. "I've been fighting with Bright and his appendix burst. I sort of needlessly bit your head off the other night and I didn't say sorry yet and I don't want you to end up in a hospital before you leave. Call me superstitious but . . . sorry."

Ephram laughed. "You are without a doubt the strangest girl I have ever met."

"I know," she agreed. "And you've been a good friend to me despite it. I have other friends— you've been different."

"Like *bad* different?" Ephram asked, worried.

"You sort of remind me of something I read in a psych class I took last summer at Everwood Community College. This experiment about two kinds of monkeys."

"I remind you of monkeys," Ephram said. "That sounds like bad different."

"Some guy raised a monkey alone in a cage with two people," Amy explained. "One guy had on a white costume, and whenever the monkey would come near him all he would do was play and tickle the monkey like crazy. The other guy in there had a black outfit and all he'd do was hug the monkey, cuddle and hug, that's it."

I think she's lost her mind, Ephram thought. "I think you've lost your mind," he said aloud.

Amy ignored him. "Most of the time the monkey hung out with the fun guy, played tickle-monkey with him for hours—I didn't know monkeys could laugh. But then out of nowhere they'd *blast* this horn and the monkey would *fly* over to the guy in black and clutch him for safety."

Ephram grinned. "Cuddle monkey."

"Right. I guess the point of the study was to show that sometimes you need one kind of monkey, sometimes you need the other." Amy spun on her stool again. "See, that's the thing. I've had people in my life who are cuddle-monkeys and people who are tickle-monkeys. But I never had a friend who was both before. Different."

In some strange way, Ephram thought that was the sweetest thing she'd ever said to him. "I guess I've been called worse," he said.

"And you totally suck for leaving," Amy added. "Did I mention that? Totally. Suck."

Now she tells me, he thought. "Actually no, I don't," he said. "I'm not going."

Amy's mouth dropped open. "You're not?" Then the words seemed to really sink in. "You're staying—for real?" she cried, a huge grin overtaking her face. "Since when?" She gave one more spin, this time flying around twice. Then she stopped and just smiled at him, the biggest, happiest smile he'd ever seen on her.

"Since after I totally embarrassed myself in front of all our family friends and told off some of the larger football players—you think that might be a problem?" Ephram stood up and began putting on his coat. All of a sudden he felt like playing in the snow.

"I thought New York had everything," Amy said.

He held open the door for her, giving her a little nudge as she walked by him. "Just about," he answered, following her out into the gorgeous Everwood winter.

CHAPTER 10

Ephram knew it was too good to last. Things had been going well for about a week. He was getting along with his dad, he and Amy were closer than ever, and he'd aced his last two tests. Then he came down to breakfast one morning to find his father on the phone, making plans to see a patient who was a few hours away.

Colin. It had to be Colin, in Denver. What other patient was that far away?

When his father hung up, Ephram raised his eyebrows in a silent question.

"That was one of the doctors from Colin's Denver team," his dad confirmed. "He's finished his basic rehabilitation."

Ephram didn't want to know what that meant, but he had to ask. "So . . . he's coming home?"

His father nodded. "A little early, if you ask me.

I'm going to Denver this afternoon. The Harts want my seal of approval."

"Great," Ephram muttered. "Be sure to tell him I said hi."

"Ephram," his dad said sympathetically. "I know this isn't easy for you."

"At least they got him back alive, right?" Ephram said. And it was true. He knew it was a miracle that Colin was well enough to come home. Another miracle at the hands of Dr. Brown. It was incredible, it was astounding, it was too good to be true. But it still sucked. It wasn't that he wanted Colin to suffer or still be in a coma. He just wanted Amy not to love him so much.

His father didn't try to talk him out of his bad mood. Neither did anyone at school. In fact no one at school talked to him at all. But throughout the day, a sense of excitement grew as the word spread that Colin was coming back. Ephram caught little bits of conversation, eyes wide, voices hushed. For the first time he really understood that through this entire thing, Amy was the only one who'd truly believed Colin would ever come back.

After school he was heading to the bike rack when he noticed a cluster of people standing nearby. He drifted over to see what was happening.

"What time?" somebody asked.

"How about balloons?" said a different voice. "Or streamers?"

Ephram pushed his way through a few kids standing at the edge of the little crowd. In the center of it all was Amy, practically bursting with joy. She raised her voice so everyone could hear her. "Okay, everybody!" she called. "If you can't bring signs or help make banners, then talk to Kayla about food. She's got a list of all the party goods the Harts requested. Also, Paige is gonna get there by five o'clock to help set up, so . . ."

Ephram turned away. He didn't need to see Amy looking like that, so . . . complete. So normal. So much like the carefree, popular girl she used to be, the girl he'd never known. He shot a glance back at her, but she still hadn't even noticed he was there. As Ephram walked away from the group of planners, Kayla popped up next to him.

"Out with the new, in with the old," she said with a sneer. "Nice *not* getting to know you." She flounced away.

Ephram wanted to make some snide comment to her, but he knew it was pointless. She was right. With Colin back, his own friendship with Amy would vanish. No matter what Amy said, that was the way it would be. They might as well be strangers.

He decided to spend the afternoon wallowing in self-pity. For an hour he lay on his bed, reading the most romantic manga stories he owned and listening to downer music at top volume. Maybe he *should* have gone back to New York after all.

Andy poked his head into the room. "We're watching *James and the Giant Peach*," he said. "Care to join us?"

"Enticing, but no."

His dad didn't leave. He just stood awkwardly in the doorway, not moving.

"Why are you doing that lingering thing you do sometimes?" Ephram asked.

"Listen, I'm not gonna force a conversation on you, but—"

"That would be a first," Ephram interrupted.

"Forget it." His father turned to go, and instantly Ephram felt bad. His dad had really been making an effort to behave like an actual human being lately, and he appreciated it.

"Sorry," he said, taking off his headphones. "What is it?"

"I was just wondering how Amy's doing," his dad said. "In regards to Colin coming home and everything."

"She's the most popular girl in school again, the love of her life is back, she's having a party. I'd say she's doing pretty good."

"A party." Ephram's father frowned. "Whose idea was that?"

"It wasn't mine, believe me. But I guess the Harts are cool with it. Half the school's planning to be there."

"I don't know if Colin is really ready for a party," his dad said, concerned. "It could be overwhelming."

"Try telling Amy that."

"Colin's a strong kid to be doing this well already, but he's not going to be the same as he was. You might need to be there for Amy, support her—"

"I don't think so. Amy and I aren't really talking much these days." *At least not since she found out Colin was coming back*, he thought.

"I'd go to the party," his dad said.

"What?" Ephram cried. "Why?"

"'Cause whatever you guys have going on won't figure itself out for a while. In the meantime, just because she stopped being your friend doesn't mean you have to stop being hers. And trust me, she's gonna need one now."

Delia called from downstairs, and his father turned and left.

Ephram watched him go, feeling a little worried in spite of himself. Sometimes he forgot that his dad actually knew Colin, that he'd seen him and spoken with him. To Ephram, Colin was just the unconscious guy in the hospital bed he'd seen a couple of times—and the reason Amy wouldn't even consider Ephram as a potential boyfriend. But his father really *knew* Colin as a person. And his father also really knew how patients recovered from brain surgery. If he said there was something to be concerned about, then he was right.

Amy will never want to believe that, Ephram thought. Which meant she was in for a nasty surprise. Which meant she'd need a friend.

Ephram heaved a sigh. He had no choice but to go to Colin's party.

It looked like a block party around Colin's house. Half the street was filled with kids holding signs and welcome-home balloons. Ephram felt a little overwhelmed by it all—he could only imagine how strange it would all seem to someone who'd seen nothing but a hospital for months. Would Colin even remember anybody? He felt a pang of pity for Colin, coming home to all these people he didn't know in a house he didn't recognize.

The Harts' car rounded the corner, and everyone cheered. They drove slowly toward the house while kids waved and called to Colin and Amy in the back seat. Colin looked kind of out of it. Then Ephram noticed Amy's face. It was a total blank. No animation at all—no smile, no loving look, nothing. Ephram's stomach gave a sickening lurch. Something was very wrong with Amy. And he suddenly knew that his father was right—she was going to need him, big-time.

Ephram hung back until the party moved inside. Colin got hugs from just about everyone, with Amy standing by his side the whole time, wearing a fake smile. Then Mr. and Mrs. Hart settled him in a chair in the corner, and people swarmed around him, talking and laughing and completely ignoring how uncomfortable Colin looked.

Somewhere in the all the bustle, Ephram lost sight of Amy. It wasn't hard to figure out where she might be. He located the Harts' back door and went outside. There she was, leaning against the house, all alone. She glanced up in surprise.

"Ephram? What are you doing here?"

"Apparently attending a party uninvited," he said, stung by her shocked tone. .

"I didn't mean it like that," she said quickly. "I'm glad you came, I just didn't think you would."

"And miss the biggest party of the winter?" he joked. "I do have a rep to maintain."

She didn't even smile. She just stared at her feet. It was worse than he'd expected. "Shouldn't you be inside being ecstatic or something?" he asked. "I mean, didn't you Martha Stewart this whole thing?"

"It hasn't really gone like I planned."

Ephram felt sorry for her. But after all, this was reality. She'd been looking forward to some kind of fairy-tale ending and it was just never going to happen. He didn't know how to help her. And he wasn't entirely sure that he was the right one to be helping her, anyway. "Colin's back," he said gently. "From where I'm standing you got everything you wanted since I met you. You should get back in there. And I should really take off."

The last thing he wanted to do was leave her when she was upset. But she had a boyfriend now—a *real* boyfriend, one who was sitting inside, barely keeping it together. Ephram wanted to do the right thing. He forced himself to turn and walk away from her.

"Hey," Amy called after him. "Can I come?"

Ephram stopped, confused. Was he supposed to say no? Hadn't he always wanted Amy to choose him over Colin just once? "Sure," he said.

They walked out the side gate and didn't speak until they made it all the way to the end of Colin's street.

"I've been wondering how you've been. I mean since before the party and all," Amy said, looking at Ephram hesitantly.

"You mean since before you were a crappy friend and disappeared on me 'cause Colin was coming home and you couldn't deal?" Ephram asked.

Amy was silent for a moment. "Yeah," she finally said. "Since then."

Ephram felt a little better. At least she wasn't doing her usual pretend-everything-is-fine routine. "I'm about the same," he told her. "I found a few new people to have lunch with at school. You might not know it but we have a non-English-speaking exchange student named Norbert. He's from Germany. Maybe Prague."

His joking worked; it made her smile. Ephram relaxed a bit. He could still make her smile. "You want to tell me what happened?" he asked.

She shrugged. "Everyone said it would be hard, seeing Colin, and no matter how many times I heard it . . . I didn't know it would be *this* hard."

"He seemed okay," Ephram said.

"You didn't know him," Amy replied. "And now he doesn't know me."

Ephram stared at his feet as they walked. So Colin didn't remember her at all. And if he didn't remember Amy, he probably didn't remember anyone at the party. Poor guy. And poor Amy.

"It's like he really did die in that accident," Amy went on. "How sad is that. I can remember what he wore on our third date, and he doesn't even know me. I built my whole life around memories of us and he can't remember my name without a cheat sheet."

Her voice broke, and Ephram didn't know what to do. His father had always said that Colin might not recover completely, not ever. But he couldn't tell Amy that.

"My dad said . . . it just takes awhile," he lied. "But he said Colin will eventually remember. You just have to stick it out."

"I've given it six months," Amy said. "When do I run out? When do I just give up?"

"You don't. That's what devotion is, Amy." Ephram

could hardly believe these words were coming out of his own mouth. "I mean, I thought you were in love with him. That's all I've heard about for the past, I don't know, *forever*. And now on the first day you throw in the towel? Truth is, you couldn't give up now even if you wanted to, because from the day I met you, you've always been loyal to Colin. And when you're loyal to someone, you can't help it. You're there for them."

And it sucks, he thought. Ephram was just as loyal to Amy as she was to Colin. And that's why he had to be there for her now, even though it was killing him. That's why he had to send her back to her boyfriend even though he wanted her to stay.

"How come you're so smart?" Amy asked softly.

"I'm not," he said. "If I was, I'd be wearing a warmer jacket." Amy smiled, and in that moment, Ephram knew he would never be more than a friend to her. It was heartbreaking. "I also wouldn't be telling you to go back to your boyfriend," he added.

"Ephram—"

"Look, I wish it was different. I wish I was here first, I do," Ephram said passionately. "But I wasn't. He needs you, Amy. He needs you to help him get better."

Amy nodded, looking up at him with tears in her eyes. Ephram knew that the tears were for *him*, not for Colin. He knew he'd just made Amy's choice for her: Colin. "I should probably get back, shouldn't I?" she whispered.

"Yeah, definitely," he told her.

"You gonna come with me?" she asked hopefully.

Ephram knew Amy wanted him to be there for her every step of the way, but he couldn't. It hurt too much. He could send her back to Colin, but he couldn't force himself to watch them together.

"I don't think so," he said.

Then he turned and walked away from Amy . . . forever.